SHREK FOREVER AFTER
THE NOVEL

BANTAM BOOKS

SHREK FOREVER AFTER: THE NOVEL
A BANTAM BOOK 978 0 553 82236 6

First published in Great Britain by Bantam,
an imprint of Random House Children's Books
A Random House Group Company

This edition published 2010

1 3 5 7 9 10 8 6 4 2

Shrek is a registered trademark of DreamWorks Animation L.L.C.
Shrek Forever After TM & © 2010 DreamWorks Animation L.L.C.

The Random House Group Limited supports the Forest Stewardship Council (FSC), the leading
international forest certification organization. All our titles that are printed on Greenpeace-
approved FSC-certified paper carry the FSC logo. Our paper procurement policy can be found at
www.rbooks.co.uk/environment.

Mixed Sources
Product group from well-managed
forests and other controlled sources
www.fsc.org Cert no. TT-COC-2139
© 1996 Forest Stewardship Council

Bantam Books are published by Random House Children's Books,
61–63 Uxbridge Road, London W5 5SA

www.**rbooks**.co.uk
www.**kids**at**random**.co.uk

Addresses for companies within The Random House Group Limited can be found at:
www.randomhouse.co.uk/offices.htm

THE RANDOM HOUSE GROUP Limited Reg. No. 954009

A CIP catalogue record for this book is available from the British Library

Printed and bound in Great Britain by CPI Bookmarque, Croydon, CR0 4TD

DreamWorks®
SHREK
FOREVER AFTER
THE NOVEL

BY LAUREN ALEXANDER

BANTAM BOOKS

Chapter One

Once upon a time, a long time ago, a king and a queen had a beautiful baby daughter. Her name was Fiona. King Harold and Queen Lilian loved their daughter. But Fiona had a terrible curse put upon her. You see, by day she was a lovely princess. By night, she was a hideous ogre.

The only way Fiona's curse could be lifted was by a kiss. This kiss could not be an ordinary kiss — one that would be given, say, by her mother or father. No, this kiss had to be given by someone who truly loved Fiona, and whom Fiona truly loved as well. Like a handsome prince in shiny armour. So Fiona waited in a tower that was guarded by a dragon until the day when her true love would arrive.

Fiona waited and waited. The days turned into months. The months turned into years. The king and

queen feared their daughter would never be rescued. They had to turn to someone for help. But who?

Finally, the king and queen were forced to resort to desperate measures. So one dark and stormy night, King Harold and Queen Lilian set out in their carriage towards a part of their kingdom they had never visited before. As they neared their destination, they peered out of the carriage window. The landscape looked strange and frightening. Witches of all shapes and sizes roamed around outside. Nervously, the queen locked of the carriage door. The king looked at his wife, desperately hoping their plan to rescue their daughter would work.

Suddenly, a bolt of lightning lit up the dark sky. A clap of thunder cut through the silence. A worried look crossed the king's face. Seeing this, the queen took his hand. Feeling a bit better, the king smiled at his wife.

Finally, their carriage came to a halt inside the gates of the Crone's Nest Carriage Park. King Harold and Queen Lilian squinted in the darkness at an egg-shaped carriage covered with signs pronouncing things like: "Magical Contracts," "Deal of a

Lifetime," and "Dreams Can Come True!"

"I don't know about this, Lilian," King Harold said nervously. "Fairy Godmother said only true love's kiss could break Fiona's curse."

Queen Lilian took her husband's hand. "I don't trust that woman, Harold. This may be our last hope. Besides, he does come highly recommended by King Midas."

King Harold shook his head. "But to put our daughter's life in the hands of this person?" He motioned to the carriage. "He's devious. He's deceitful. He's . . ."

"Rumpelstiltskin!" announced the strange little man inside the carriage, welcoming them in.

Cautiously, King Harold and Queen Lilian walked inside. Rumpelstiltskin hopped off his chair and kissed the queen's hand. "Mrs. Highness," he said.

A shiver ran down Queen Lilian's spine as she eyed the little man. "How do you do?" she finally managed to say.

Just then a goose appeared, greeting the king and queen with a loud hiss.

"Down, Fifi, get down!" Rumpelstiltskin shouted

at the bird. Then Rumpelstiltskin placed a piece of crumpled paper on the desk. "As you can see, everything's in order," he said.

King Harold looked at the contract.

"So you'll put an end to our daughter's curse?" King Harold asked.

Rumpelstiltskin nodded, rubbing his tiny hands together. "And in return," he said, "you sign the kingdom of Far Far Away over to me."

A bolt of lightning cracked, lighting up the carriage with an eerie glow.

King Harold turned to his wife. "Lilian," he whispered, "this is madness!"

Queen Lilian nodded her head. But the desperate look in her eye told her husband that this was their only hope. "What choice do we have, Harold? Fiona has been locked away in the tower far too long," she whispered.

"It's not like she's getting any younger," Rumpel butted in.

King Harold looked at the contract. He had a nagging feeling that something just wasn't right. "But to sign over our *entire* kingdom!" he exclaimed.

Rumpelstiltskin shrugged his little shoulders. "Well, if your kingdom is worth more than your daughter . . ." Without finishing his sentence, he reached a teensy finger over to the contract and began to slide it off the desk.

"Nothing is worth more to us than our daughter," King Harold stated, firmly putting his hand on the contract.

The queen grabbed her husband's hand. She knew they were making the right decision. What good was an entire kingdom without their daughter?

"I knew you'd see things my way," Rumpelstiltskin said with a sly grin. And with that, he reached for a bottle of magic ink and closed the window shutters.

"Jump, Fifi, jump," Rumpel commanded.

Fifi leaped into her master's arms. Rumpelstiltskin gently petted her soft down, then yanked out one of her tail feathers.

"Honk!" Fifi shouted in surprise.

Rumpelstiltskin dipped the feather quill into the pot of magic ink and handed it to the king. The king took the quill and slowly, ever so slowly, moved it towards the contract.

Suddenly the door burst open. A breathless royal messenger burst inside. "Your Highness! The princess! She's been saved!" he cried.

The king and queen looked at each other. They were elated! At long last, their daughter had found true love. Quickly, the king tore the contract up into shreds and the royal couple exited the carriage, leaving Rumpel alone and dumbfounded. He didn't understand — how had his plan gone awry so quickly?

But Princess Fiona had indeed been saved — and by an ogre named Shrek, who came to be loved and revered throughout Far Far Away.

Meanwhile, as Rumpelstiltskin's life deteriorated, he plotted his revenge. He pledged that, one day, he would get back at Shrek and take over the kingdom of Far Far Away!

Years passed, and Rumpelstiltskin still held his grudge. One afternoon, in a bookstore, Rumpel picked up a storybook that told the tale of Shrek and Fiona's love story. Disgusted, he leafed through the pages, reading aloud to no one in particular. "True love's kiss led to marriage and ogre babies!" he said, ripping out a page from the book.

"And the kingdom of Far Far Away was finally at peace," Rumpelstiltskin continued, tearing out another page. "Oh, goodie for them!" he added, rolling his eyes.

"And they lived happily" — *RIP!* — "ever" — *RIP!* — "after!" Rumpelstiltskin shouted, ripping out page after page.

"Uh, sir," a bookstore employee said. "You're going to have to pay for that."

Rumpelstiltskin spun around and eyed the employee. It was Pinocchio.

"Maybe we can make a deal for it, little boy," Rumpel said, his eyes glowing.

"Oh, I'm not a real boy," Pinocchio said.

"Do you want to be?" Rumpelstiltskin asked. "What do you say, Pinocchio?"

"Nobody needs your deals any more!" Pinocchio shouted. And with that, he tossed Rumpel right out of the store!

Rumpelstiltskin was furious. "I wish that ogre was never born!" he shouted.

Chapter
Two

But Shrek was indeed born, and he was living his life happily ever after with Fiona, and their three children: Fergus, Farkle, and Felicia.

"Wake up, Daddy, wake up!" Felicia shouted one morning, squeezing her favourite toy, Sir Squeakles, in Shrek's face.

Shrek and Fiona turned over in bed and smiled at each other.

"Good morning," Fiona said lovingly to her husband.

"Good morning to you," Shrek answered, giving his wife a kiss.

Shrek and Fiona got out of bed and started their morning routine. Shrek sat in the living room feeding the babies while Fiona did the laundry.

One after the other, each of the babies let out a

satisfied burp.

"Better out than in," Fiona said, smiling at her family.

"That's my line," Shrek said with a laugh.

After the babies were fed, Shrek brought Fergus to the changing table. It was time to change someone's dirty nappy.

As Shrek pulled off little Fergus's nappy, he was in for a smelly surprise. "Did my little Fergus make a — *whoa* — big, grown-up ogre stink?!" Shrek exclaimed.

After the dirty business was done, Shrek walked outside to deposit the disgusting nappy into the nappy pail.

"Oh, that's diabolical," Shrek said, wrinkling his nose. "Whew!"

Then it was time for Shrek to take a well-deserved bathroom break. He grabbed a newspaper and headed for the outhouse.

Just then, a Star Tours chariot full of tourists arrived in front of Shrek's house.

"And on your left lives the loveable lug that showed us you don't have to change your undies to change

the world," the gnome tour guide announced into his megaphone.

Annoyed at the gnome's intrusion, Shrek stormed into his outhouse and slammed the door.

"Wonder what Shrek's up to in there," joked the gnome over the loudspeaker.

As the day went on, so did Shrek's fatherly duties.

"Get in . . ." Shrek fretted as he tried to get a shoe onto Farkle's squirming foot. "Impossible to put on . . ." he grumbled.

Just as Shrek was about to give up in frustration, Fiona arrived, easily sliding the shoe onto Farkle's foot.

"OK, the dragon goes under the bridge, through the loop, and finally, into the castle," Fiona recited, as she tied the shoelace. Farkle stood up between his parents, and to his delight, they blew raspberry kisses on his cheeks as he giggled.

Later in the day, Shrek managed to steal a few quiet moments for himself. He mixed an eyeball-tini and sat back on his favourite chair to relax in, when . . .

"Playdate!" Donkey shouted, popping his head into the window.

13

"Ah!" yelled Shrek, sitting up.

Before Shrek had a chance to react any further, his front door burst open.

In came Donkey with his five dronkey children.

Shrek's brief moment of relaxation was over.

The afternoon playdate led to a dinner date — complete with Shrek, Fiona, the three ogre babies, Puss In Boots, Donkey, Dragon, and the dronkeys. Around the dinner table that night, Puss told the story of how Shrek and Fiona met.

"Then Shrek kissed the princess," Puss said with a dramatic flourish. "She turned into a beautiful ogre, and they lived . . ."

"Happily," Donkey said popping up between Shrek and Fiona.

"Ever," added Fiona with a loving smile.

"After!" Shrek concluded.

Everyone cheered and clapped. "Hooray!" they all shouted.

Later that night, after all the guests had left and the babies were put to bed, there was still more work to be done. Shrek cleared the dining room table while Fiona washed the dishes in the sink.

"Look," Fiona said to Shrek, pointing to the sky. "A shooting star."

She closed her eyes, crossed her fingers, scrunched up her nose, and made a wish.

"So, what did you wish for?" Shrek asked his wife.

"That every day could be like this one," Fiona replied with a soft smile.

Shrek snuggled up to his true love. "Ah, come here, you."

And with that, he gave his true love a kiss.

Chapter Three

Fiona's wish did indeed come true. Every day was just like the last one. Every day, the ogre babies stood at Shrek's side of the bed and woke him up, ready for breakfast. Every day, Shrek fed and changed the babies, and Fiona did the laundry. And every day, the gnome tour guide passed Shrek's house and told the tourists, "This loveable lug taught us you don't have to change your undies to change the world!"

And whenever Shrek tried to relax with an eyeball-tini, Donkey burst through the door with his dronkey children, ready for their playdate. Even when Shrek tried to enjoy the smallest pleasures in his life — like a mud bath, for example — his fatherly and husbandly duties would call . . .

"Shrek, the outhouse is clogged up!" Fiona would shout.

And each night at dinner, Puss would recount the story of how Fiona and Shrek met, and tell all about their "happily ever after" ending.

Winter came with lots of snow, yet Shrek's daily routine remained the same. Spring came and rain poured down, yet Shrek's days stayed the same. And when the season changed again, this time to summer, everything in Shrek's life remained — you guessed it — the same.

One night, after the guests had left and the babies were put to bed and the dishes were all washed and dried, Shrek lay in bed. He stared at the ceiling, listening to Fiona snore.

Shrek thought about his day. Wake up! Burp! Poop! Playdate! Mud bath! Outhouse! Happily. Ever. After.

After a while, certain that sleep would not come, Shrek got out of bed. He walked over to his dresser, opened a drawer, and pulled out a worn, folded piece of paper. It was an "Ogre Wanted" poster.

Smoothing out the creases, Shrek stuck the poster in the corner of his mirror. He looked at the ogre in the picture. Then he looked at his reflection in the

mirror. Shrek roared a tiny roar. That didn't sound like the fierce ogre he had once been. Shrek let out a bigger roar. *Pathetic*, he thought with a sigh.

Chapter
Four

Shrek woke up the next morning in the usual way. He was ready for another day of the same old, same old. But then he realized that this day would be different. It was the babies' first birthday!

Donkey and Dragon and their dronkey kids arrived early to whisk Shrek and his family off to town. Everyone climbed onto Dragon, and off they flew. They were having a party at the Candy Apple with all their friends and family.

"Nice landing, baby," Donkey told Dragon as they reached their destination. "Now remember, don't eat the valet," he reminded his wife.

Dragon snorted in response.

Fiona placed her babies on the dronkeys' backs and they flew off towards the party.

Just then, Puss In Boots strolled by, his arms full of

gifts. "Happy birthday, niños," he called to the babies as they flew off. "Vamos a la fiesta," he said, heading into the party.

Shrek watched Puss leave and shook his head. Puss was off to the party, but Shrek wondered if *he'd* ever get there with all the baby gear he had to carry.

"Woohoo! Shrek! Shrek!" a group of villagers called out as Shrek struggled to close the babies' pushchair.

Surprised, he turned to see a group of villagers carrying torches and pitchforks. Was this like the good old days, when he was a feared ogre?

No such luck.

"Oh, Mr. Shrek, would you sign our pitchforks?" one of the villagers asked.

"And our torches?" another villager asked, lighting up his flame in Shrek's face.

"Oh man," a third villager said, shaking his head. "You used to be so fierce."

"Yeah, when you were a real ogre," another villager agreed.

"A real ogre?" Shrek asked incredulously.

Ouch, that hurt.

Finally, Shrek made it to the birthday bash. He looked around the Candy Apple, a bright and colourful family-fun centre. He couldn't believe that this place had once been the Poison Apple, the joint he and the other villains had loved to frequent when he was a "real ogre." An animatronics band had replaced the old piano. And a unicorn ride sat where there was once a bucking bronco.

Shrek stood miserably in the crowd of guests, watching Pinocchio sing with the animatronics band onstage.

"Happy birthday bash, no more nappy rash. One year older not a pain, friends still remain the same . . . refrain!" Pinocchio sang at the top of his wooden lungs. "Super duper, party pooper, birthday bash, birthday bash, birthday bash . . ."

"Birthday bash! Dah dah dah dah dah!" everyone in the crowd joined in.

Everyone, that is, except for Shrek.

"Man, this song never gets old!" Donkey commented, obviously enjoying himself.

Squeak! Felicia squeaked Sir Squeakles in her father's ear.

"Please, Felicia, not in Daddy's ear," Shrek said, plucking the toy from her hand and stuffing it into his vest pocket.

Just then, a villager dad and his son approached Shrek.

"Excuse me, Mr. Shrek? I'm Lemke, and this here is my son, Butter Pants. Could you do that ogre roar of yours for my son? He's a big fan."

Shrek looked down at the chubby-cheeked Butter Pants.

"Do the roar!" Butter Pants shouted impatiently.

Shrek shook his head. "You know, I'd rather not. It's my kids' birthday party and . . ."

"Do the roar!" Butter Pants demanded.

Thankfully, Fiona walked up to them just then. "Uh, honey, why don't you go check on the cake?"

"Sure," Shrek agreed, breathing a sigh of relief.

"And don't forget the candles," Fiona reminded him.

Shrek headed off to the bakery counter, where Muffin Man was busy adding some decorative frosting to Gingy.

"Hold still," said Muffin Man, adding a couple of

last-minute icing flourishes.

"Thanks for the pants, Muffin Man!" Gingy said. He stood up to look at Muffin Man's handy work. Although he had trousers painted on the front of his legs, the backs of his legs were bare!

But Gingy seemed excited. "I always wanted chaps!" he said with a smile.

Then Muffin Man gave him a little cowboy hat to complete his cowboy look.

"Yeehaw! Giddy up! Rawhide!" Gingy shouted, dancing around.

When Muffin Man looked up, he saw that Shrek had arrived at his counter.

"Ah, Monsieur Shrek!" Muffin Man shouted a greeting.

"Howdy, Shrek!" Gingy said with a tip of his hat.

Muffin Man reached down under the counter and proudly presented Shrek with the birthday cake.

Shrek glanced at the cake. A hideous, smiley-faced iced ogre stared up at him.

"Oh, what is that supposed to be?" Shrek asked.

"That's Sprinkles the Ogre!" Gingy replied.

Just then, Donkey appeared by Shrek's side. "Aw,

Shrek, it's a party! Cheer up," he told his friend.

"I'm in a great mood, actually," Shrek said, seething with anger.

But Donkey didn't register the tone in Shrek's voice. Instead, he looked at the cake. "Ooh!" he exclaimed. "I'm going to lick me a rainbow!" And with that, he shoved his face into the cake box.

If Shrek wasn't angry enough before, now he was furious. Donkey had just ruined his babies' birthday cake. "Donkey!" he shouted.

Then Lemke and his annoying little son chose that moment to walk right up to them.

"As long as you're not doing anything, how about one of those famous Shrek roars?" Lemke asked.

"Do the roar!" Butter Pants begged.

Shrek was starting to fume. "Let me set you straight, Butter Pants," he said. "An ogre only roars when he's angry. You don't want to see me angry, do you?"

"Do it," Butter Pants insisted.

Shrek took a deep breath, picked up the cake, and simply walked away. "Hold it together. Just hold it together," he said to himself.

"Daddy, he's getting away," Butter Pants whined. "Do something."

Back at the party, Shrek dropped the freshly tongue-smeared cake onto the table in front of Fiona.

"Oh, good," Fiona started. Then she took a look at the cake and gasped. "What happened to the cake?"

Shrek looked at the cake. With the tongue smear on the top, he could no longer make out the happy ogre face. "Trust me, it's an improvement," he told her.

"Ugh, you licked it," Queen Lilian said in disgust.

"No," Shrek stated.

"Just because you are an ogre doesn't mean you have to eat like one," Queen Lilian said.

To make matters worse, Shrek had forgotten the birthday candles. Fiona hurried off to get the candles. As she did, she cautioned Shrek to watch the cake. But when he looked back at the table, the cake was gone!

"Ah! Where's the cake?" Shrek shouted.

"Vee ate the cake," one of the Three Pigs admitted.

"Ya," a second pig agreed.

"What?" Shrek said.

In the midst of all the commotion, the babies began to cry.

"No, don't cry. Shhh," Shrek said soothingly.

Just then, Lemke and Butter Pants appeared again.

"Hey, I believe you promised my son a roar," Lemke said.

Shrek's head was spinning. Roar! Cake! Disaster! Shrek was really starting to seethe. He had just about had it!

But Donkey still wasn't picking up on his friend's frustration. "Hey, everybody," he announced. "Shrek's going to do his famous ogre roar!"

"Not now, Donkey!" Shrek warned.

Slowly, a crowd began to form around Shrek.

"Pigs, are there any cupcakes?" Shrek asked, trying to concentrate on the task at hand.

"Vee ate them, too," the second pig admitted.

"Zey have lollipops," the first pig offered.

"No, I ate them," the third pig confessed.

The second pig was outraged. "Vat? You didn't share?"

"Well, you didn't share the croissants!" the third pig said.

All the while, the ogre babies were becoming hysterical.

"Everything's going to be OK," Shrek said to his sobbing babies.

Just then, Fiona returned to see the empty cake box and the children crying. "Shrek! What's going on?" she exclaimed.

But before Shrek had a chance to explain, Donkey cut in. "Come on, Shrek! Your fans are waiting!"

The crowd egged him on; they really wanted to hear the famous roar. And on top of that, Fiona was nagging him about the cake.

The crowd's faces began to blur and swirl around him. The children were wailing. The crowd was chanting. Finally . . .

"*Rooooooaaaaaaaaarrrrr!*"

Shrek roared with such force that half the crowd got knocked over.

Everyone was in complete and total shock. That is, until they all erupted in cheers. "Shrek! Shrek! Shrek!" they cried excitedly.

"I love you, Daddy," Butter Pants beamed to his father, glad to have got his roar.

"I have found another cake," Puss In Boots announced.

Shrek looked at the new cake. That stupid, adorable ogre face was once again beaming out at him. That was it! He couldn't take it any more.

Wham! Shrek furiously slammed his fist through the cake.

Stunned silence filled the room.

Not knowing what else to do, Shrek stormed out of the Candy Apple, slamming the door behind him.

He breathed in the night air, happy to be alone in the alley.

Only . . . he was not.

Rumpelstiltskin was there, hiding behind some rubbish bins. The odd little man had been scavenging through the garbage when he had seen Shrek and jumped out of sight.

A moment later, Fiona stepped out the back door, looking for Shrek. "Unbelievable," she said, shaking her head.

"Tell me about it," Shrek agreed. "Those villagers

are . . ."

"I'm not talking about the villagers, Shrek," Fiona interrupted. "I'm talking about you. Is this really how you want to remember the kids' first birthday?"

Shrek was exasperated. "Oh, great, so this is all my fault?" he said.

"Yes," Fiona said with a nod. "But let's talk about this at home, after the party."

"You mean that roadside attraction we live in?!" Shrek was growing upset again. "Step right up! See the dancing ogre! Don't worry, he won't bite," Shrek said, mimicking the tour guide gnome.

"I used to be an ogre," Shrek continued angrily. "Now I'm just a jolly, green joke."

"OK, OK," Fiona said gently. "Maybe you're not the ogre you used to be. But maybe that's not such a bad thing."

"Ah, I wouldn't expect you to understand," Shrek shot back. "It's not like you're a real ogre. You spent half your life in a palace."

Fiona was stung. "And the other half of my life was spent locked away in a tower," she reminded him, with a hurt tone in her voice.

"Look, all I want is for things to go back to the way they used to be," Shrek tried to explain. "Back when villagers were afraid of me and I could take a mud bath in peace. When I could do what I wanted, when I wanted to do it. Back when the world made sense."

"You mean back before you rescued me from the Dragon's Keep?"

"Exactly!" Shrek shouted.

Fiona's face crumpled. Wasn't he happy with the life he had with *her*? Wasn't he happy being a father?

"Shrek, you have three beautiful children, a wife who loves you, friends who adore you. You have everything. Why is it that the only person who can't see that is you?"

And with that, Fiona turned and walked back to the door. But before she went inside, she looked to see if Shrek was coming with her.

But he just stood still.

So Fiona left Shrek where he wanted to be — alone.

Little did she know, Shrek wasn't alone at all. Rumpelstiltskin was still there. From his hiding place behind the rubbish bins he had heard every word. And he liked what he had heard. Rumpel grinned a nasty little grin. He had a plan.

Chapter

Five

Shrek was still fuming. There was no way he was going back into the party to tell Fiona how sorry he was. How could Fiona not realize that he had to have some time of his own — some *Shrek* time? Right now, a walk through the forest was just what he needed.

"If she thinks I'm going to slink back there and apologize, she's got another thing coming," Shrek grumbled to himself. "She's not the boss of me. I'm an ogre! And I'm not going to apologize for acting like one."

Suddenly, Shrek heard someone cry out.

"Help!" a man shouted. "Please, someone, anyone! Oh, help me! Please help!"

Shrek's ears perked up. Who was crying out?

Shrek walked down a dirt road, spotting an

odd-looking carriage with a broken wheel. A large goose was attached to the front of the vehicle where a horse would normally be. And sticking out from underneath the carriage were two curly-toed shoes!

"I'm stuck! Oh, help! Oh, please help!" the voice shouted. "Someone, anyone! Oh, help me! The pain! I can see a bright light, a tunnel . . ."

Shrek cautiously went to help whoever was beneath the carriage. He leaned down and lifted up the vehicle.

It was Rumpelstiltskin! Though of course Shrek didn't know that — yet.

"Grandma? Is that you?" Rumpel asked.

"Yeah, it's me — or — Granny," Shrek said, playing along. He looked at the little man lying before him, thinking he must be in shock from the accident.

Rumpelstiltskin looked up at Shrek, his eyes widening in horror. "An ogre!" he shouted, scrambling even further beneath the carriage. "Oh, please, mister ogre, please don't eat me," Rumpel said.

Shrek shook his head. "I'm not going to eat you."

Cautiously, the little man peered up at Shrek.

"But, but, you are an ogre, aren't you?" he stuttered.

"Yeah, well, I used to be," Shrek said. "Look, move out or get crushed."

Rumpelstiltskin crawled out from under the carriage. Shrek swiftly spun Rumpel's spare wheel into place and set the carriage back down on the ground.

"So you're not going to eat me?" Rumpel asked.

Shrek shook his head. "No, thanks. I already had a big bowl of curly-toed weirdo for breakfast." And with that, Shrek started back on his walk.

"Hey, hey, hey, wait up!" Rumpelstiltskin called out after him. "What's your rush? Where are you going?"

"Nowhere," Shrek answered truthfully.

The little man cracked a smile. "What a coincidence! I was just heading that way myself," he chuckled. "But seriously, let me give you a ride. I insist!"

Shrek looked down at the strange man. He didn't quite know what to make of him. Plus, all he really wanted to do right now was be alone. He really didn't want to spend his evening with this oddball.

"Come on, it's the least I can do after all you've done for me," Rumpel urged. "I've got a hot rat cooking," he added, knowing that would tempt Shrek.

It worked. Shrek climbed into the carriage, and off they went. The little man tried his best to hide his excitement — so far, everything was going exactly as he had planned!

Rumpelstiltskin tried to make his guest feel at home. "All right! So can I interest you in a mudslide? Slug and tonic? A liquid libation to ease that frustration? Huh?" The little man poured his concoction into a glass and shook it with force.

"Eyeball-tini?" he offered Shrek.

Shrek couldn't resist. "Well, maybe just one."

Shrek and Rumpelstiltskin enjoyed their drinks while Fifi pulled the carriage down the road. As their journey progressed, the two chatted like two old friends, sharing jokes and telling stories.

"I've got to say, Shrek," said Rumpel finally. "I envy you. To live the life of an ogre. No worries, no responsibilities. You are free to pillage and terrorize as you please."

"Free? Ho-ho, that's a laugh," Shrek scoffed.

"Oh yeah?" Rumpelstiltskin asked. He wanted to hear more.

"Sometimes I wish I had just one day to feel like a real ogre again," Shrek told him.

Upon hearing this, Rumpelstiltskin perked up. "Well, why didn't you say so? Magical transactions are my speciality!"

"Oh great," Shrek said sarcastically. "Next to mimes, magicians are my favourite people."

Rumpelstiltskin went over to a shelf and began to rifle through a stack of papers. "King for a Month. Knight for a Week," he said tossing the papers aside. Then, he found what he was looking for. "Ogre for a Day." He presented the contract to Shrek.

"Think about it, Shrek. To be feared and hated. You'll be like 'Roar!' and the villagers will be like 'Ah! Get away from me! It's Shrek! I'm so scared of him!' It'll be just like the good old days. When your swamp was your castle. When the world made sense . . ."

For a moment, Shrek was caught up in what Rumpelstiltskin was saying. It *did* sound ideal. Then, he snapped back to reality.

"All right, what's the catch?" he asked.

"Catch? No, there's no catch," Rumpel said, trying to sound innocent. "No catchings, really. I mean, there's something, small thing. A little thing."

Shrek was starting to get annoyed. "All right, I knew it. So what do you want?"

"A day," Rumpelstiltskin admitted.

"A day?" Shrek asked, confused.

Before Rumpelstiltskin could answer, the oven timer went off. The rat was done. Pulling on a pair of tiny oven gloves, Rumpel pulled the rat roast out of the oven. Shrek's mouth began to water. But he knew he had to get back to the matter at hand. His stomach could wait. For a bit. He looked at Rumpelstiltskin.

"Well, to make the magic work, you've got to give something to get something. In this case, you've got to give a day to get a day. That's all," Rumpelstiltskin explained.

Shrek wasn't sure if he could trust the little man. He eyed the contract uncertainly.

"I can't just pick up and leave my family," Shrek told him.

"Oh, but that's the best part, Shrek," Rumpel

said. "It's a magical contract. No one will even know you're gone! And by the time this day is up, you are going to feel like a changed ogre."

That sounded better to Shrek. Still, he wasn't one hundred percent sure.

"So what day would I have to give up?" Shrek asked.

"Oh, I don't know," Rumpelstiltskin said casually. He poured gravy over the rat, trying to distract Shrek. "A day from your past. How about a day you had the flu? A day you lost a pet?" He turned his back to Shrek, and started to saw through the roasted rat. "A day some meddling oaf stuck his big nose where it didn't belong, destroying your business and ruining your life!"

Crack! Rumpelstiltskin's knife went through the rat and split the plate in two! Shrek raised an eyebrow at Rumpel.

"Just for an example," Rumpel said with an innocent smile. He presented the sliced rat to Shrek.

"How about the day I met Donkey? Now there's a day I'd like to take back," Shrek said with a laugh.

Rumpelstiltskin joined in with raucous laughter,

and then stopped abruptly. "I don't know who that is," he said seriously. Then he continued. "I know! What about a day you wouldn't even remember? Like a day when you were a baby! An innocent, mindless little baby."

"Take any of those days you want. Take them all for all I care," Shrek said, taking a bite of rat.

Rumpelstiltskin's beady little eyes lit up. "Oh, just one will do."

And with that, the evil little man scrawled some words on the contract with a magic quill.

"OK, good!" Rumpel said, lifting the quill from the paper. "A day from your childhood it is!"

Shrek thought about it for a minute. Should he do it? He was just giving up one day after all. And it was a day in his life he didn't even remember. What could possibly go wrong? This deal seemed too good to pass up.

"I guess there's nothing wrong with wanting a little time for myself," Shrek mused.

"It's just twenty-four tiny, little hours," Rumpelstiltskin said, rubbing his tiny hands together.

Shrek was starting to get excited. "I'm still my own ogre," he said.

"Yes you is!" Rumpel agreed.

"I never needed to ask for anyone's permission before," Shrek reasoned.

"So why start now?" Rumpel asked.

Shrek took the quill from Rumpel. This guy might be a little, well, *unusual.* But he was right. Shrek didn't need anyone's permission to trade one little day in his life. And he'd get to be an ogre for a day. Not the kind of ogre he'd been lately, but the kind of ogre that was feared across the land.

Rumpelstiltskin tried to remain calm as Shrek's hand hovered over the contract. But his nerves were getting the best of him. Sweat dripped from his head. His toes curled. This could be it. This could be what he had been waiting for!

Hardly able to contain himself, Rumpel began to mutter, "Go on, Shrek, sign it! Go on, Shrek, sign it! Sign it, Shrek, sign it!"

Finally, Shrek inked his name on the contract.

"Oh, you signed it," said Rumpel.

"So tell me," said Shrek, "what happens now?"

"Have a nice day!" Rumpelstiltskin said with a laugh.

Poof! Rumpelstiltskin vanished in a puff of golden smoke, his carriage disappearing along with him. Just like magic!

Chapter Six

Shrek landed on the ground with a hard thud. The sun was rising. Confused, he looked around to find himself sitting in the middle of a forest path, the contract still in his hand.

Suddenly, he heard a familiar voice coming down the forest path. It was that obnoxious gnome tour guide and his Star Tours chariot filled with tourists, headed his way.

"Oh, great," Shrek muttered as the chariot rolled closer and closer.

"And as we head over the river and through the woods, we come across . . ."

"An ogre!" a tourist cried, spotting Shrek.

Everyone on board screamed, scared for their lives. Frantically, the Star Tours chariot tried to speed away. Faster and faster it drove, until — *Crash!* The vehicle

smashed into a tree. Terrified, the tourists jumped off the chariot and scampered in all directions.

Dumbstruck, Shrek stared at the scene that had just unfolded before him. Were these the same tourists that came by his swamp each day, eager to hear about how he didn't have to change his undies to change the world?

Then Shrek's eyes fell upon Rumpelstiltskin's contract. With a laugh, he realized that Rumpel's "Ogre for a Day" promise had become a reality. Shrek gleefully kissed the contract. This was going to be the most perfect day!

Shrek walked down the road, eager to see what kind of terror he could stir up. He sauntered towards a village and passed under a sign that read "Pleasure Fair." *Perfect!* Shrek thought.

As Shrek passed a group of villagers, they screamed and ran away. Shrek smiled to himself. He didn't even have to roar, and they were scared stiff!

Up ahead, he spotted a crowd watching a puppet show. In the show, a villager puppet was beating up an ogre puppet.

"Kill that ogre! Kill that ogre!" the crowd cried.

Sensing a perfect entrance, Shrek snuck up behind the puppets, then jumped up with a huge roar.

"Aaah!" the villagers shouted, running away. Shrek laughed and moved on for more fun.

Inside a church, a bride and groom stood at the altar.

"You may kiss the bride," the priest announced, concluding the ceremony.

The groom leaned in to kiss the bride, expecting to be met by a pair of soft lips. Instead, he found Shrek's face before him! Horrified, the groom let out a scream and ran. Then Shrek turned and roared at the wedding guests. Everybody fled for their lives.

Shrek looked at the empty church, feeling pleased with himself. He spun around in pure joy. It felt so good to be a feared ogre again!

Energized, Shrek ran outside. He ferociously roared at a couple having a romantic picnic.

They tossed their food into the air and ran away as fast as they could. Then he roared at a cat. It hissed. Then at a mirror. It cracked. Then he roared at a goose. It laid an egg. Shrek thought, *what's next?*

Quietly he crept up to a grocer who was piling watermelons. Crouching down, Shrek put his green head next to the fruit. As the grocer reached for Shrek's watermelon-like head, he popped up. "Roar!" Shrek cried.

The villagers had had enough of this terrorizing. "Filthy ogre!" they cried, chasing him through the town.

But Shrek didn't mind. He was having too much fun! Thinking fast, he grabbed hold of a tavern sign and scrambled with it up to a rooftop.

Then he hopped on top of the sign as though it were a surfboard and glided down the thatched roofs of the town's buildings. *Woohoo!* Shrek thought, riding from rooftop to rooftop.

Suddenly, Shrek ran out of roofs. He catapulted himself into the air, landing in a hay cart.

The villagers gathered around him, pitchforks and flaming torches in hand.

"This is the part where you run away!" Shrek shouted in joy.

And with that, the frightened villagers fled.

Shrek leaped off the hay cart, did a cannonball in

midair, and landed right in the middle of a pool of mud.

Shrek heaved a big sigh. This was the life!

🍄🍄🍄

Later that day, as Shrek walked through the forest, he came upon an "Ogre Wanted" sign tacked to a tree. It was identical to the one that he had hidden in his drawer.

"Oh, sure is great to be wanted again," Shrek said with a laugh. "Oooh, nice one."

Shrek looked around. His wanted posters were tacked up on every tree — just like old times!

Then he spied a poster that did not have his face on it. It was an ogre all right, but this one had long, red hair.

"Fiona?" Shrek whispered as he neared the poster.

He looked around again. Sure enough, he was surrounded by dozens of posters with Fiona's face splashed on them. His wife was a wanted ogre? If Fiona was on the run, then where were Fergus, Farkle, and Felicia? Were they in danger? Shrek had to find out!

Chapter

Seven

Shrek ran to his swamp. Breathing hard, sweat dripping from his brow, he frantically looked around. All he saw was the large tree stump that used to be his home. But it looked as though no one had ever lived here. There was no door. There were no windows.

"Fiona!" Shrek shouted for his wife. But his voice was carried away by the wind.

Shrek felt around the tree stump. Maybe this was some kind of joke. Perhaps there was a secret opening somewhere, one that would lead him inside his house and back to his family.

"Fiona! Are you in there?" Shrek cried, banging on the stump.

Bang! Bang! Bang! Shrek pounded the hollow tree stump with all his might. Finally, he broke through.

Then Shrek heard a noise. Quickly, he cleared away a bunch of vines. Maybe his bedroom was behind this mess. Maybe he'd find Fiona curled up in bed with his three little children. But once Shrek cleared the growth, all he found was a bunch of rats.

Shrek ran outside. "All right, Rumpel," he cried. "This wasn't part of the deal!" Shrek waited for a response. Nothing.

"Rumpel!" Shrek cried again, only to be met once again by silence.

Shrek did not understand what was happening to him. This wasn't supposed to be part of the deal. Shrek pulled Rumpelstiltskin's contract out of his pocket and studied it. But the words before him didn't make sense.

Suddenly, a bright orange flash crossed the sky above his head.

Zoom!

Shrek looked up, but couldn't make out anything.

Zoom! Zoom! Zoom! Flashes of orange streaked the sky again.

Frantically, Shrek searched the sky for the source

of the noise. At last, one of the streaks slowed down — it was a witch flying on her broom!

"Ogre!" one of the witches shouted. She and three other witches hovered over Shrek's head. Shrek looked up at them, annoyed.

"We've got another one, ladies," one of the witches shouted. "Get him!"

The witches let out a unified cackle.

"Who are you?!" Shrek shouted at the witches. "What are you doing in my swamp?"

One of the witches swooped down towards Shrek. Stepping out of her path, Shrek grabbed her broom and sent her flying into a tree.

"Looks like a troublemaker," another witch said as her group continued to circle around Shrek's head.

A third witch grabbed an apple from her cauldron, bit off the stem, and threw it towards Shrek. The apple hit Shrek on the head and bounced harmlessly to his feet.

But just as the apple hit the ground — *poof!* — it exploded into a cloud of purple smoke. Shrek coughed, batting at the smoke furiously.

Just as the air began to clear, one of the witches

clamped a skull handcuff onto Shrek's left arm. Desperately, he tried to pull his arm away, but it was no use — the handcuff was chained to the witch's broom.

Before he could consider what to do next, the witches snapped two more skull handcuffs onto his legs.

Then one of the witches shouted an order, and they flew off on their brooms, carrying Shrek into the air.

"Whoa!" shouted Shrek as he was pulled off the ground.

Once more, Shrek tried to free himself. As he shook and shimmied around, the witches wobbled on their brooms. Then — *crash!* — Shrek smashed into the ground.

But the witches weren't about to give up. They continued to fly, even as Shrek bumped and skidded along the dirt. Finally, they managed to lift the big ogre up into the air.

Up, up, up they flew.

"You witches are making a big mistake," Shrek shouted at them. "I know my rights!"

"You have the right to shut your mouth!" one of the witches shouted back. With that, she tossed a pumpkin bomb in Shrek's direction. It exploded into a cloud of smoke.

With one breath of the pumpkin bomb's fumes, Shrek's world went black.

Chapter Eight

When Shrek woke up, he heard a familiar voice singing a song about tomorrow.

"Donkey, stop the singing, will you?" he asked. But the song kept going.

Shrek groggily opened his eyes, confused by his unfamiliar surroundings. Where was he? He tried to sit up.

Wham! His head smashed into a wooden ceiling. Shrek rubbed his head, looking around. He was inside a caged carriage . . .

. . . and Donkey was pulling it!

Only it didn't look exactly like his dapper old friend — this Donkey was a scruffy, ungroomed mess.

"Donkey, where am I?" Shrek asked. "What's happening?"

"Quiet down there!" someone shouted.

Shrek looked up and saw two witches riding on top of the cage.

Donkey continued singing.

"Oh, I hate this song!" one of the witches shouted, cracking her whip across Donkey's back.

Quickly, Donkey changed his tune and sang another song. But the witch didn't like this one, either, and whipped him again.

Frustrated, Donkey said, "Will you witches make up your mind, please?"

But the witches just lashed the whip once more.

Finally, Donkey found a song they all liked. As they all sang, Shrek whispered, "Psst, Donkey, what's going on? Do you know where Fiona is?"

"Shh. Quiet, ogre," Donkey shot back. "You're going to get me in trouble and I need this job. I am not going back to work for Old MacDonald. Tell me to E-I-E-I-O. 'E-I-E-I-NO!' That's what I said."

Shrek didn't know what Donkey was talking about. All he wanted was to find out where his family was. "Where are my babies?" Shrek asked. "And where's your wife, Dragon?" Shrek asked.

"Look, ogre," Donkey said. "I think you must

have me confused with some other talking donkey. I've never seen you before in my life."

Shrek couldn't believe what Donkey was saying.

"Never seen me before?" Shrek asked incredulously. "Come on, Donkey."

"Hey, and how do you know my name, anyway?" Donkey asked.

"It's me, Shrek," he shouted. "Your best friend!"

Donkey let out a whoop. "A donkey and ogre, friends!" he chuckled. "That's the most ridiculous thing I've ever heard."

Shrek sighed. He peered out from the bars of the cage to try to figure out where he was. But he had no idea.

"Can you at least tell me where they're taking me?" Shrek asked.

"To the same place they take every ogre," Donkey told him. "To Rumpelstiltskin."

Shrek's eyes narrowed. "Stiltskin," he muttered angrily. He should have known that Rumpel was up to no good.

Shrek pushed his face up closer to the bars, as the now barren landscape of Far Far Away unfolded

before him. His eyes widened with horror.

"Oh no," he whispered.

Up ahead, on the hillside, the letters of the Far Far Away sign were burned and falling down. The once-thriving city below was a pile of rubble and ruins. In the distance sat a giant, fancy-looking, egg-shaped palace where the old castle had been.

As Shrek was wheeled through town, he passed a group of peasants gathered in a circle. They were watching some sort of fight taking place. Muffin Man was there. He seemed to be organizing the group.

"It's time to crumble!" Muffin Man cried out to the crowd. "Come on, place your bets. Place your bets!"

Then Muffin Man pulled out a spatula with a biscuit on top of it. Shrek watched as the biscuit flipped itself upright, leaped from the edge of the biscuit tool, and soared through the air. Deftly, it landed in the middle of the circle, poised to fight.

Who was this fearless warrior? Shrek squinted to get a closer look.

It was Gingy!

But Gingy wasn't the sweet, little gingerbread

boy Shrek knew. He was a tough-looking gladiator biscuit. And he was ready for battle!

Just then, a group of animal crackers came charging out of their box. Gingy charged the crackers head-on, slicing them to crumbs with his lollipop scythe.

"Gingy snap!" Gingy cried, as he snapped off an animal cracker's head.

Shrek stared in disbelief as his cage rolled past.

Then, out of nowhere, a wad of garbage hit Shrek in the head!

"There's one!" an angry peasant cried. "Hideous monster! Get him out of here! Filthy ogre! Disgusting creature!"

The surrounding villagers hurled more and more garbage at Shrek. He tried to duck out of the way of the flying trash as his cage-carriage was pulled inside the palace walls.

Once inside, Shrek saw a line of ogres tied together by chains, toiling away at work. Evil witches stood nearby, whipping the ogres to work harder. Ogres as slaves? Shrek was sad. And ashamed. Was this all his doing?

Chapter Nine

Finally, the carriage came to a stop in the courtyard. Once again, metal cuffs were clamped around Shrek's wrists and neck. Connected to the cuffs were chains. And pulling the chains was a group of witches, eager to prove they were in control of Shrek.

As Shrek was dragged away, he leaned down to Donkey and whispered, "Don't worry, Donkey, I'll get us our lives back."

"Yeah, right," Donkey shot back. "Put a little mustard on mine, Captain Crazy."

The witches were pulling Shrek towards the palace, when suddenly the doors swung open. Inside, music pulsed and witches danced under a huge disco ball. As Shrek looked around, he saw the Three Pigs serving pork to a goose. Shrek recognized that goose! It was Rumpel's pet goose, Fifi.

Shrek's eyes found the evil little man seated at a table with a group of witches. His feet were up, a drink was in his hand, and he wore a smug smile on his face.

Then a witch walked up to the table, announcing that Rumpelstiltskin had a customer.

"Wolfie!" Rumpel shouted. "Bring me my business wig."

Wolfie ran up to his master and placed a business-like wig on Rumpel's head.

Pinocchio stepped up to Rumpel, who laid one of his contracts on the table. "Terms are in the details, balsa boy," Rumpelstiltskin said.

Pinocchio was elated. At last, he would be turned into a real boy. "Sayonara, termites. Hello, acne!" he exclaimed.

But just as Pinocchio was about to sign the contract, Shrek yelled out, "Stiltskin!"

"Oh! Shrek!" Rumpelstiltskin said with a laugh. "There he is."

Rumpel leaped from the table, spilling the magic ink all over Pinocchio's contract, and blotting out his signature.

"No!" the wooden puppet cried out. "So close!" And with that, the witches led him away.

"Have I been waiting for you!" Rumpel said to Shrek. Then he turned to the room. "Ladies, this is the guy that made all this possible," he announced.

Rumpel walked over to the shackled Shrek. "So, tell me, how are you enjoying your day?"

Shrek was enraged. He wasn't going to play Rumpel's game. "All right, Rumpel," he said. "What's going on? What have you done?"

Rumpelstiltskin shook his head. "Oh no, Shrek, it's not what *I've* done. It's what *you've* done. Thanks to you, the king and queen signed their kingdom over to me."

"They would never do that," said Shrek.

"They would have done anything if they thought it would end their daughter's curse," explained Rumpel.

"I ended Fiona's curse!" Shrek shouted.

Rumpel smiled. "How could you when you never existed?"

"You better start making sense, you dirty little man," Shrek said.

Rumpel reached into Shrek's pocket and pulled out their contract. "Here, let me spell it out for you," Rumpelstiltskin explained. "You gave me a day from your past. A day you wouldn't even remember. A day when you were an innocent, mindless baby," he said.

Shrek was shocked. All the pieces were starting to come together. "You took the day I was born," he stated.

Rumpelstiltskin shook his head. "No, Shrek, you gave it to me."

Shrek's face tightened with fury. "Enjoy this while you can, Stiltskin. Because when this day is up . . ."

"But, but, but, but," Rumpel interrupted. "You haven't heard the best part. Since you were never born, once this day comes to an end," he pointed to his hourglass, "so will you!"

Nearby, a witch cackled as she flew over to the table and set down a giant hourglass.

"Where's Fiona?" Shrek shouted angrily. "Where's my family?!"

Rumpel laughed. "Silly little ogre. You don't get it, do you? You see, you were never born. You never met Fiona. Your kids don't exist."

Shrek was speechless. What had he done? The room spun around him.

"Happy ogre day!" Rumpelstiltskin announced with glee.

Shrek was irate. With an anger he hadn't felt in ages, Shrek burst through his chains, easily shaking off the witches that were holding him.

Rumpel jumped behind the massive hourglass for protection. "Get him, get him, witches!" he cried.

Meanwhile, Donkey was standing outside the throne room doors with a bunch of witches. "You know what would help morale around here?" Donkey said to them. "Flip-flop Fridays. Feet all comfortable with the breeze on your toes . . ."

Blam! Shrek burst through the door, interrupting Donkey's little speech.

"Whoa!" Shrek shouted as he soared through the doors on a stolen witch's broom.

Donkey stared as Shrek rode the broom, chased by a squadron of witches. The cackling witches chased Shrek through Rumpel's massive hall of pillars. In, out, and around and around the pillars Shrek flew.

"Lock all the doors, you worthless witches!"

Rumpelstiltskin cried, running out of the throne room.

"I'll be right back, Donkey!" Shrek cried as he flew past his friend's head.

"I don't know you!" Donkey yelled at Shrek.

Turning to Rumpel, Donkey again stated, "I don't know him."

The witches were in hot pursuit of Shrek. They rode as fast as they could, throwing flaming pumpkin bombs at Shrek, hoping to knock him down.

Finally, after gaining a bit of distance, Shrek headed back towards the throne room. Swooping up above the landing where Rumpel stood, Shrek stared down at his enemy.

"I'm glad I'm not you," Donkey said to Rumpelstiltskin.

Rumpel cowered behind his witches. Was he about to meet his end?

Suddenly, Shrek swooped down and grabbed — Donkey!

"No! Ahh! Help me!" Donkey cried as he flew off with Shrek.

The pair flew into the throne room, the witches

at their tail. Shrek looked up and saw the giant disco ball hanging from the glass-domed ceiling above him. He had an idea!

Pulling on his broom, Shrek headed up towards the glass ball. Grabbing the ball by its chain, Shrek and Donkey burst through the glass ceiling, jamming the disco ball into the hole in the ceiling they had created. The pursuing witches flew straight into the ball!

Shrek and Donkey were free!

Rumpelstiltskin stared as his giant disco ball fell onto the floor with a huge smash.

"Wolfie!" Rumpel screamed. "My angry wig!"

Seething in anger, Rumpelstiltskin slapped a fiery red wig on his head, swearing silently to find Shrek and bring him back.

Chapter Ten

Shrek and Donkey flew for miles on the stolen broomstick.

"Help! Ogre!" Donkey shouted as they wobbled on the out-of-control stick. "I've been kidnapped by a deranged, unbalanced ogre! Help!" He kicked and shoved Shrek.

"Donkey! Get off of me!" Shrek told him urgently. "Watch it with your pointy hooves!"

Suddenly they dropped lower into a row of trees, crash-landing to a stop. As soon as they hit the ground, Donkey took off running.

"Hey!" Shrek called after him.

"Just take my wallet!" a petrified Donkey shouted. "Just take my wallet! I'm being ass-napped!"

"Donkey!" Shrek yelled, tackling his friend to

stop him from running away.

"Help!" Donkey shouted again. "Animal cruelty! Help . . ."

Shrek cupped his hand over Donkey's mouth. "You need to calm down," he told him. "I'm your friend."

Donkey mumbled something behind Shrek's hand.

"I'm not going to hurt you, all right?" Shrek continued.

Donkey nodded. He seemed to understand Shrek.

But as soon as Shrek took his hand from Donkey's mouth, Donkey shouted, "Please, please eat my face last and send my hooves to my mama!"

"Donkey, you've got to trust me," Shrek implored.

"Why should I trust you?" Donkey asked, terrified.

Shrek was frustrated. How could he possibly convince Donkey that he could be trusted? Suddenly Shrek had an idea.

Shrek began to sing a song that Donkey used to

sing when the two of them were actually friends.

But this just freaked Donkey out even more.

"Whaa!" he shouted, running away.

Shrek gave up. It was useless; he'd never convince Donkey that he was a friend. "Fine, go ahead, run away! Who needs you?" he called out.

Angrily, Shrek sat down on a tree root.

Squeak! Shrek heard a noise.

He reached into his pocket and dug out Sir Squeakles, his daughter Felicia's toy. *Felicia*, Shrek thought. *Farkle, Fergus, Fiona.* What had he done to his beloved family by signing that contract with Rumpelstiltskin? Slowly, a tear escaped from his eye and rolled down his cheek.

"I've never seen an ogre cry," Shrek heard Donkey say.

Shrek looked up. Donkey had returned to his side. "I'm not crying," Shrek stated.

"It's nothing to be ashamed of," Donkey told him. "I mean, I cry all the time. Just thinking about my grandma. Or thinking about kittens. Or my grandma kissing a baby kitten. Or a little baby grandma kitten." Donkey stopped talking and

started to cry. "This is so darn sad."

"I said I'm not crying!" Shrek shouted.

"Hey, take it easy, I'm only trying to help. None of my business why you're upset," Donkey said. "By the way, why are you upset?"

Shrek told Donkey that he was tricked into signing something that he shouldn't have signed. He pulled out Rumpel's contract and showed it to Donkey.

Donkey gasped. "You should never sign a contract with Rumpelstiltskin," he said, stating the obvious.

"Yeah, I know that," Shrek said.

"His fine print is crafty," Donkey told Shrek, who nodded.

"And his exit clauses are sneaky!" Donkey added.

Shrek's ears perked up. *Exit clauses?*

Donkey explained how people get out of Rumpel's contracts. "Used to be you had to guess his name, but now everybody knows who Rumpelstiltskin is."

"Donkey," Shrek stated, "I've read the fine print and there's nothing about an exit clause in here."

"Well, you didn't expect him to make it easy for you," said Donkey, taking the contract from Shrek and folding the paper with his hooves.

Shrek looked at Donkey, puzzled.

"I didn't spend all that time around those witches without picking up a few tricks," he told Shrek.

Shrek watched as Donkey cleverly folded the words and sentences like origami.

"Your tiny, little ogre brain couldn't begin to comprehend the complexity of my polygonic foldability skills," Donkey stated.

"What are you doing?" Shrek asked, leaning closer to Donkey.

"OK, here's what you've got to do," Donkey said, still folding. "You fold this piece here, make this letter match up there, bring this corner over here like this, and if you do it just right, it will show you what to do!"

Finally, he finished folding the contract. "There!" Donkey announced. "Try Lou's Bliss!" Now, it was Donkey's turn to be confused. "Who is Lou?" he asked Shrek.

Frustrated, Shrek snatched the contract from

Donkey and began folding it himself. After a minute, Shrek revealed the words: "True love's kiss." Shrek looked up at Donkey with a smile.

"Well, you're going to have to take me to dinner first," Donkey told him.

Shrek shook his head and read the fine print written along the edge of the folded contract. "According to fairytale law, if not fully satisfied, true love's kiss will render this contract null and void."

Shrek's face brightened. "Donkey, you did it!" Shrek shouted, picking up his friend.

Spinning Donkey around, Shrek explained, "If Fiona and I share true love's kiss, I will get my life back!"

"OK, OK," Donkey said, wriggling out of Shrek's arms. "This isn't a petting zoo. So where is this Fiona?"

"Well, that's just it," Shrek told him. "I don't know."

"You know, when I lose something, I always try to retrace my steps," Donkey said. "So, where did you leave her last?"

A wave of panic hit Shrek. "The last time I saw

her, I told her I wished I'd never rescued her!"

Shrek knew what he had to do. Without wasting another minute, Shrek took off for the Dragon's Keep. When he finally neared the tower, everything was dark and eerily quiet. The flowing lava that had once surrounded the Dragon's Keep had hardened to a black volcanic shell. Frantically, Shrek ran across the rope bridge. He had to reach the tower, and fast!

"Shrek! Shrek!" Donkey called after him. "Are you crazy? That's the Dragon's Keep! They keep dragons in there!"

As Donkey struggled to keep up with Shrek, his hoof suddenly broke through one of the slats of the bridge. Petrified, Donkey scampered back to solid ground.

"OK, yeah, fine. Go ahead," Donkey shouted ahead to Shrek. "I'm going to just hang back here and find us some breakfast!"

Shrek ignored Donkey and kept on running. He raced into the Dragon's Keep and sprinted up the winding staircase of the tallest tower. Reaching Fiona's chamber, he swung open the door.

"Fiona!" Shrek shouted.

But the room was empty. Fiona was nowhere to be found. All that was left in the room was a bunch of cobwebs and dust.

Desperately, Shrek scanned the room. On one wall, he saw some markings. Pulling aside a dusty curtain, he saw more etchings. Fiona had been counting something, but what? Suddenly, Shrek realized that she must have been keeping track of the days she was kept as a prisoner inside the Dragon's Keep. The days that had passed because Shrek had never rescued her!

Shrek turned to Fiona's bed. On it sat Fiona's princess tiara. Shrek picked up the crown. "If I didn't save Fiona, then where is she?" he asked aloud.

Shrek was beginning to lose hope.

In despair, Shrek looked down at the dirty floor. His eyes fell upon something white. Picking it up, he realized it was the handkerchief that Fiona had given him when he rescued her. But in this twisted reality he was currently in, he never *did* rescue her. And he never got the handkerchief.

Shrek picked up the favour and stuffed it in his pocket. Then he moved to the tower window and looked out at the horizon. He thought about how lonely Fiona must have been all those years in the tower. His heart bled as he thought about his beloved Fiona waiting for him. And how he had let her down.

But if Shrek had not rescued her, where had she gone?

Chapter Eleven

While Shrek was in the Dragon's Keep, Rumpelstiltskin was sitting inside his conference room. He was fuming. How could his band of witches have let Shrek get away?

But he wasn't about to give up. He'd capture the ogre, no matter what.

"Some people like to look at the goblet as half empty," Rumpel said with a sigh. "Me, I like to look at it as half full." He looked up and stared at the witches that sat around the large conference table.

"We've gone from the bottom to the top, ladies," he continued. "But we're not just an empire, we're a family."

Then, swiftly, Rumpel changed the subject. "Everyone's got their cupcakes?" he asked. "Cupcake? Cupcake?"

Satisfied that the cupcakes had been distributed, Rumpel stood up and walked behind the seated witches, popping his head between them as he spoke. "You know we have put away a lot of ogres. And so one got away?" he shrugged. "Who cares? It's not a big deal. Doesn't matter to me. It's not like it's the end of the world."

The witches nodded in agreement. Maybe they were going to get off the hook!

Then, suddenly, Rumpel hopped up on the table. "Except, funny thing, now that I think about it, the ogre who got away is *Shrek*," Rumpel said, getting more agitated. "And if he shares a kiss with Fiona by sunrise, well, it *is* the end of the world. *Our* world! *My empire*!" By this point, he was shouting hysterically.

Rumpelstiltskin took a deep breath. He knew he needed a clear head in order to track down Shrek and maintain rule of Far Far Away.

"But as I was saying," Rumpel continued. "I like to look at the goblet as half full."

He reached over for a jug of water and a glass. But he was so preoccupied that the glass started to overflow. Seeing this, the witches gasped in terror, afraid that the spilling water might melt them.

"Would anyone care for some water?" Rumpel threatened the witches. "Wet your whistle? A clear, crisp, delicious glass of agua purificada? Anybody thirsty?"

Rumpel looked around at the petrified group. "Nobody's thirsty? Well then, does anyone care to tell me what it's going to take to get this ogre?" Rumpel pointed to a witch. "You?"

"Faster brooms?" a witch named Amber suggested.

"No," Rumpel said.

"Pointier hats?" Griselda piped up.

"No!" Rumpel shouted, pointing at another witch.

"Maybe we could hire a professional bounty hunter?" the witch said.

"No!!" Rumpel was furious. What was wrong with this group? He tossed his glass of water in the witch's face.

Instantly, the witch began to melt! "What a world . . . what a world . . ." she mumbled as she got smaller and smaller. And then — she was gone!

"Hmm . . . you know, actually, not a bad idea," Rumpel said scratching his chin. Then he called for his head witch, Baba.

Nervously, Baba stood up. What was Rumpel going to do to her? She eyed the water jug. Would these be her last moments on Earth?

"I need a bounty hunter," Rumpel told Baba. "And if music doth soothe the savage beast, then I think I might know just the person."

Rumpelstiltskin was pleased. He had a plan, and he was sure it was going to work. He'd capture Shrek before Shrek and Fiona could share that kiss. Then the empire would be his — forever!

Chapter Twelve

Back in the forest outside the Dragon's Keep, Shrek stood before Donkey, holding Fiona's handkerchief.

"This is the favour Fiona was supposed to give me on the day we met," he told Donkey. "It's a symbol of our love. Now smell it," he said sticking the handkerchief in front of Donkey's nose.

"Hey, man, get that dirty old favour out of my face," Donkey said, batting the handkerchief out of the way.

"*Your* nose is the only chance I have of tracking down *my* wife," Shrek told Donkey. "Smell it! Get it! Away you go, girl!"

Donkey pushed Shrek away. "Do I look like a bloodhound to you? In case you haven't noticed, I'm a donkey, not a dog. If I was a dog, they'd call me

'Dog' not 'Donkey' and . . ."

Donkey stopped talking. His nostrils flared. He had picked up the scent of something. It smelled sweet. And luscious. And tasty. Donkey had to find the source of the smell. He took off, charging through the woods.

Filled with hope, Shrek followed Donkey — only to be led to a plate of waffles, sitting in the middle of the forest!

"And I thought the Waffle Fairy was just a bedtime story," Donkey said as he walked towards the steaming plate of delicious-looking food.

Donkey stuck out his tongue, ready to take a lick of syrup.

"Donkey!" Shrek shouted before Donkey could reach the sweet, sticky syrup. "Don't eat that!"

But Donkey couldn't resist. It just looked *so* good. And he hadn't eaten anything in *so* long. His tongue edged closer to the waffles.

"There's a stack of freshly-made waffles sitting in the middle of the forest. Don't you find that a wee bit suspicious?" Shrek reasoned.

Donkey considered what Shrek said for a minute.

And then he licked the waffles.

But as soon as Donkey's tongue left the waffles — *splat!* — the plate flew up against a tree, revealing a hole in the ground right in front of his hooves!

"Uh-oh!" Donkey said, looking down into the big hole.

Just then, from behind Shrek's head, a log swung down. Shrek desperately tried to warn Donkey, but he was too late. The log knocked Donkey down the hole.

Shrek raced over to the hole that had swallowed up his friend. As he peered down into the darkness, he saw Donkey lying there, twenty feet below.

"Donkey! Are you OK?" Shrek called.

"I'm fine," Donkey replied.

But as soon as the words left his mouth, a rope looped around his tail and yanked him away.

Donkey was gone.

Chapter Thirteen

Shrek couldn't believe his eyes. Donkey had disappeared. Frantically, Shrek jumped into the hole. *Thud*! He landed hard at the bottom. He looked around. Where was he? And more importantly, where was Donkey?

Just then, Shrek spotted a small opening a few yards away from where he had landed. And it looked as though the opening led to some sort of tunnel. Shrek ran to the opening, got down on all fours, and started to crawl through it.

"Help, help me! Help, Shrek!" came Donkey's voice through the tunnel.

Shrek crawled faster and faster, desperate to reach his friend. Finally, he saw another opening, and he climbed through it. And when Shrek emerged through the opening, he was amazed at what was before him.

A huge army of ogres was going about their business in a camouflaged bundle of tents. The camp held more ogres than he'd ever seen — fat ogres, ugly ogres, tall ogres, small ogres, gross ogres. It was an amazing sight!

"Hey, it's a new guy!" one of the ogres shouted, pointing at Shrek.

"All dressed up in his Sunday vest," another ogre commented.

"He's really tiny, isn't he?" a third ogre said.

Then a serious-looking ogre spoke up. "Fate has delivered us a comrade-in-arms, and for that we are grateful! Suit him up!"

And with that, the ogres pulled Shrek to his feet. Shrek tried to protest, but the ogre soldiers wouldn't listen to him. The ogres bathed Shrek in buckets of mud. Then, quicker than Shrek could burp, they fitted him for armour — wrist gauntlets, a chest plate, and everything a soldier would need. They seemed satisfied with their work.

"Here you go," a general said to Shrek as he dropped a battleaxe into his hands.

Shrek was incredibly confused. And before he could

ask any questions, the ogres that had been attending to him suddenly ran screaming into attack mode, spears flying through the air. Shrek's heart began to race.

But as he looked around, he saw that the spears were landing in witch dummies. It appeared to be some sort of training session.

"Welcome to the resistance," an ogre said, walking up to Shrek.

Shrek was puzzled. "Resistance?" he asked.

"We fight for freedom, and ogres everywhere," the ogre replied. Then he reached up to his nose and blew, making his ears trumpet like battle horns: *toot-toot-a-toot.*

"Good one, Brogan!" the ogres shouted as they tooted back in response.

"I didn't know we could do that," Shrek said, amazed.

Suddenly, Shrek heard a cry for help coming from across the camp. It was Donkey! And he was tied by his legs onto a cooking spit. It looked like Donkey was about to become tonight's dinner!

"You can't eat me. I got the mange! I'm poisonous!" Donkey pleaded as two ogres carried him towards a fire.

To shut him up, one of the ogres carrying him quickly stuffed an apple into his mouth.

Shrek raced over to Donkey. "Uh, this order's to go," he told the ogres, hoping they would let his friend free. "Trust me," he added. "You don't want to eat this one."

"I go down smooth, but I come out fighting," Donkey put in.

Shrek saw that the ogres weren't going to let Donkey go, so he grabbed the spit. Frantically, he tried to pry it out of their hands. But the ogres held on tight.

Back and forth they pushed and pulled, until suddenly, everything stopped. Everyone was still, and deadly quiet.

Slowly, Shrek looked around. In the near distance, standing atop a hill, stood what appeared to be the ogres' leader. Shrek watched as the ogre, dressed in full battle gear, removed his battle helmet, and shook out a mane of long, flowing hair.

Wait a minute — the leader wasn't a *he*, it was a *she*.

And it was *Fiona*!

Chapter Fourteen

"Fiona!" Shrek shouted, as he raced towards his wife.

But instead of being greeted by her soft lips, he was greeted by her hard foot!

Bam! Shrek flew through the air, landing with a thud at the feet of the other ogres.

Fiona walked over to Shrek, who was rubbing his aching jaw, and stood over him menacingly.

"For future reference, personal space is very important to me," Fiona said, glaring at Shrek.

"You don't know who I am, do you?" Shrek asked.

Fiona shook her head, and immediately turned away and began barking orders at the ogres.

"Brogan, I have news from Far Far Away. Gather the others and meet me in the war room," Fiona

said.

"Fiona . . ." Shrek said, desperately trying to get her attention.

But Fiona just ignored him. "Gretched, make sure everyone is prepared to move out tonight," she commanded.

"Fiona, I need to talk to you," Shrek pressed.

"What is it?" an annoyed Fiona said.

"OK, I know you don't remember me, but we're married," Shrek began. "And at the birthday party with some pigs and a puppet, the villagers and this boy kept saying, 'Do the roar! Do the roar!' Then I punched the cake that the pigs ate, and the next thing I knew, my donkey fell in your waffle hole."

Fiona shook her head in disbelief. "Whoa, I guess I must have kicked him harder than I thought."

"Fiona, I need to . . ."

But Shrek didn't get a chance to finish his sentence, because at that moment, a band of cackling witches swooped overhead.

"Witches!" Fiona shouted. "All right, everyone, you know the drill."

"Witches?!" Donkey cried. "Oh no, witches,

witches!"

Quickly, Shrek untied his friend, slapped his hand over his snout, and whisked him off to safety.

Shrek and Donkey watched as the ogre army snapped into action. In a matter of seconds, the entire camp was camouflaged. As the squadron of witches flew overhead, they didn't see the army or the camp. The ogres were safe — for now.

"Fiona, that's the third patrol today. We can't hide forever," Brogan said.

"Trust me, Brogan," Fiona said as she and the ogres walked away. "After tonight, we won't have to."

Shrek and Donkey watched Fiona and her crew disappear into a hollowed-out tree. It looked like some sort of meeting room, or war room — a place where they planned their strategy.

"That's your wife?" Donkey asked Shrek, shaking his head.

"That's my wife," Shrek answered.

"Well, I see who wears the chain mail in your family," Donkey joked.

Shrek ignored the comment, and walked over to

the tree. As he peered through an opening, he could see Fiona and her troops gathered around a model of a battlefield. She was explaining her plan to them. Rumpelstiltskin was planning to personally lead tonight's ogre hunt. This was good news because he'd be out in the open and more vulnerable, and easier to attack!

"The plan's simple," Fiona said reaching for a model of Rumpel's carriage and his witches. "If they follow the usual patrol route, they'll reach the river by midnight."

"We'll be concealed along this road, waiting for his caravan," Fiona continued, pointing to ogre models hiding in the hills overlooking the carriage's path.

Slowly, Fiona rolled the carriage into an open area of the map. "Once they reach the clearing, I'll give the signal and then we attack!"

Fiona moved the model ogres into attack mode, surrounding the carriage.

"And when the smoke clears . . ." Fiona paused. "Wait a minute — what's this?" she said pointing to something that clearly didn't belong.

"That's my chimichanga stand," piped up the

ogres' chef.

"Um, no, Cookie, we won't be needing that," Fiona told him.

"Trust me, Fiona, you all are going to be really hungry after this ambush, OK?" Cookie said. "Go on and finish your little speech."

Fiona shook her head and continued. "All right, as I was saying, when the smoke clears, Rumpelstiltskin is gone, and the chimichangas have been eaten, Far Far Away will finally be free! Now spread the word. We move out as soon as Rumpel leaves the palace."

The meeting was over, and Donkey and Shrek quickly pulled their heads away from the opening.

"Man, this is serious," Donkey said.

"Tell me about it," Shrek agreed. "How am I ever going to get her to kiss me before sunrise?"

Donkey cleared his throat. "Actually, I was talking about the revolution."

Shrek just waved him off. Revolution, shmevolution! The most important thing going on here was that he needed to get his wife — and his life — back!

From the look on Shrek's face, Donkey could tell

what he was thinking. "Why don't you just tell her what you told me? You know, about how you're her true love and you came from an alternate universe," he suggested.

"Oh, and while I'm at it, why don't I tell her that you're married to a fire-breathing dragon and you have little mutant donkey-dragon babies?"

"I do?" Donkey asked, shocked.

Shrek sighed. "You saw what happened. She's going to think I'm crazy."

"I'm a daddy?" Donkey said, still in disbelief.

Shrek sat down, and tried to think of a plan. As he stared at the ground, a frog hopped by. Shrek picked it up and said, "But you know what? If I got Fiona to kiss me once . . ." He took a deep breath, blew the frog into a balloon, smiled at Donkey, and concluded:

". . . then I can do it again!"

Chapter

Fifteen

Shrek was determined to win Fiona's kiss. Later that evening, he grabbed his frog balloon, tied it to a basket of gifts, and headed over to her tent with Donkey in tow. Maybe, Shrek thought, the sight of him carrying this present would melt her heart. Well, it was worth a try. Shrek stood outside Fiona's tent and took a deep breath.

"Shrek, do my babies have hooves or talons?" Donkey asked, breaking Shrek's concentration.

"Donkey, shh," Shrek said.

Shrek stepped inside the tent and looked around. The place was filled with weapons, maps, battle armor, and animal fur.

"Hello? Fiona?" Shrek called.

Then he spotted something in a corner. It was a cat. But this wasn't any ordinary cat. It was a fancy-

looking cat with a purple bow, sitting in a fancy-looking cat condo.

"You should not be here, señor," the cat told Shrek.

Shrek looked at the cat and gasped. He would know that little Spanish accent anywhere. It was Puss In Boots — minus the boots, sword, and hat!

"You've got to be kidding me," Shrek said, looking this chubby new Puss up and down.

Puss slid down the side of his cat condo and landed on a fluffy pillow. "Feed me, if you dare," he said to Shrek with what he hoped was a menacing look.

"Puss, what happened to you? You got so, so — fancy," Shrek said.

"Do I know you?" Puss asked, confused.

"Where's your hat? Where's your belt? Your wee little boots?" Shrek continued.

"Boots? For a cat? No!" Puss said incredulously.

"But you're Puss In Boots," Shrek insisted.

"Maybe once," Puss agreed sadly. "But that is a name I have outgrown."

"That's not the only thing you have outgrown," Shrek muttered.

91

"Hey!" Puss said defensively. "I may have let myself go a little since retirement, but hanging up my sword was the best decision of my life. I have all the cream I can drink and all the mice I can chase."

Just then, a mouse scurried up to Puss's bowl of milk and took a drink. The lazy Puss didn't even try to go after the mouse. "Eh, I'll get him later," he said.

But Shrek doubted he could catch the mouse even if he wanted to. Poor Puss was a just a fat, spoiled house cat now. Shrek felt personally to blame for Puss's sorry state.

"Oh, Puss," sighed Shrek. "What have I done to you? You've gone soft."

"Well, I do get brushed twice a day," admitted Puss, who simply yawned and settled happily into his fluffy pillow.

"Look, it's not too late to fix it," Shrek told him. "All you have to do is help me get a kiss from Fiona and . . ."

"What are you doing?" Shrek heard Fiona's voice say. When he turned, he saw Fiona standing by the tent door. Shrek turned a deep shade of green.

"Can I help you with something?" Fiona asked.

"Well, I know how stressful mounting a rebellion can be — rallying the troops, planning the attack — so I brought you a little something to ease the tension," Shrek said, showing Fiona his gift basket with the frog balloon tied to it.

"A gift basket?" Fiona asked incredulously.

Shrek smiled. "You're welcome," he said. "So, let's see what you've got."

He dug through the basket and pulled out a heart-shaped box of slugs and a skunk-scented candle. Also in the basket was a book of hand-drawn coupons. One was good for a free foot massage. Another was for a mud facial. And a third was for — one free kiss.

"Let's cash this coupon in now," Shrek told Fiona, hopeful that just one kiss would be all it took to return them to their normal lives.

Shrek leaned forward and puckered up. Fiona held out her arm to stop him.

"Look, I don't know what this is all about, but I'm trying to run a revolution," Fiona said seriously. "So unless you have Rumpelstiltskin's head in there, I suggest you take your gift basket, get out of my tent,

and go make yourself useful."

"Wow," Shrek said, nodding. "You're right. I am sorry. I was just trying to be friendly. No hard feelings?"

He extended his hand, and Fiona shook it. But Shrek wasn't about to leave without that kiss. He pulled her in for a hug, and then tried to sneak in a smooch. Before their lips could meet, Fiona twisted Shrek's arm behind his back, led him to the door, and tossed him outside.

Once Shrek was gone, Fiona turned to Puss. "Where did we find that guy?" she asked.

Puss didn't answer Fiona. He was too busy looking at himself in the mirror — his pink bow, his pudgy stomach.

"Could it be true?" he asked Fiona. "Have the years of prim and pampery made me soft?"

Fiona brushed off his comment. "Don't be silly," she said, pulling out a hairbrush. "Now who's a pretty kitty?" she asked.

"I am," Puss answered with a grin. Being pampered wasn't so bad, after all.

Puss wasn't the only one getting groomed. Back at the golden-egg palace of Far Far away, Rumpelstiltskin's goose, Fifi, was getting some attention of her own.

Fifi opened her mouth as one of the Three Pigs reached in and brushed her teeth. The second little pig clipped Fifi's claws, while the third little pig cleaned under her wings.

"Daddy thinks you look real nice," a satisfied Rumpel said.

Then Rumpel turned to the pigs. "All right, piggies, be gone. And don't forget to take her little potty box with you."

The first and second little pigs used all their might to lift the large litter box, and the third little pig sprayed perfume over them. As they tried to leave, Fifi grabbed the third little pig's curly tail with her beak.

"Ooh, zis little piggy wants to go home," he complained.

Then a few witches entered the throne room.

"Mr. Stiltskin! He's here," one of the witches, named Griselda, announced.

"Nice," Rumpel said with an evil little grin.

Rumpelstiltskin looked towards the door, where a man playing the flute was being carried in on the backs of a horde of rats. As he played, the rats lowered him to the ground and scattered.

"Pied Piper," Rumpel acknowledged the man. "How was your commute?"

Pied Piper tooted his flute.

"You call this guy a bounty hunter?" Griselda asked with a laugh. "What's he going to do, flute those ogres a lullaby?"

Rumpel didn't answer Griselda. Instead, he just gave the Pied Piper a little nod. In response, the Pied Piper flipped through his flute settings. He passed *rat* and *unicorn*, and finally settled upon *witch*.

The Pied Piper put the flute up to his mouth and started playing. Instantly, Griselda started to dance against her will. She started slowly, but then she burst out into a break dance. The other witches joined in.

Rumpel laughed and grinned at the Piper's power. "All right, that's enough," he finally told the Pied Piper.

As soon as the Piper tooted his final note, the

King Harold and Queen Lilian almost sign
away their kingdom to Rumpelstiltskin.

Pinocchio kicks Rumpel out of the bookstore
for destroying books.

Rumpel catches Shrek during a weak moment.

Shrek signs Rumpel's Ogre for a Day contract.

Shrek returns home to find his swamp empty.

Meanwhile, Rumpel's witches are on ogre patrol!

Shrek is captured and taken to see the new king of Far Far Away—Rumpel.

Gingy is a fierce gladiator in Rumpel's kingdom.

Shrek escapes Rumpel's castle on one of the witches' brooms.

Luckily, true love's kiss will break Rumpel's contract.

Shrek convinces Donkey to go on an adventure with him.

So the two friends set
out to find Fiona . . .

. . . but she is nowhere to be found.

Shrek tries to stop Donkey from eating a stack of waffles. It could be a trap!

Puss In Boots is now Puss In Bows!

Shrek tries to woo Fiona but is quickly rejected.
What will he do now?

exhausted witches stopped dancing.

"Looks like it's time to pay the Piper," Rumpel told the witches.

The witches just stared at Rumpel.

"Griselda, seriously," he yelled at one of his witches. "It's time to pay the Piper! Now go get my cheque book!"

Rumpel was pleased. The Pied Piper had proven that he could do the job — and well. He turned the setting on his flute to ogre and waited for his orders from Rumpel.

Chapter

Sixteen

Back at the ogre camp, the ogres were getting ready to eat dinner. Shrek walked into the kitchen and saw Cookie, the ogres' chef, standing in front of a big pot.

"Here!" Cookie said, shoving a pot into Shrek's arms. "Make sure they eat up. You can't end tyranny on an empty stomach. Go on now," he urged, pushing Shrek out of the kitchen.

Shrek walked over to the group of hungry ogres and served them their dinner. The eyeball soup smelled good, but Shrek had no appetite. He was still thinking about Fiona and how to win her over.

Donkey, on the other hand, didn't seem at all concerned about Shrek's situation. As usual, he was enjoying being the centre of attention, entertaining the ogres. Donkey dipped his nose in a bowl of soup,

and when he lifted up his head, eyeballs were stuck in his nostrils!

The ogres roared with laughter.

"That's quite a friend you've got there," Brogan said to Shrek. "I can see why you haven't eaten him."

Shrek just rolled his eyes. "Donkey," he said. "I hate to pull you away from your adoring public, but I'm not getting anywhere with Fiona. I need your help."

Before Donkey could respond, Cookie walked up to the table with a box of heart-shaped slugs. It was the same box of heart-shaped slugs that Shrek had given Fiona.

"Who wants dessert?" Cookie asked the group.

As the ogres tore into the food, Shrek's heart sank.

"Where did you get these?" one of the ogres asked as he munched.

"Fiona's garbage. Just another gift from some clueless lover boy," Cookie said.

Shrek cringed. He tried to get Donkey's attention. "Donkey, what am I going to do? It's like I don't even know her."

Donkey shook his head. "You're in trouble,

Romeo, because the only thing Fiona cares about is her cause."

"To the cause!" Brogan shouted, overhearing Donkey.

"To the cause!" the other ogres echoed, raising their glasses.

Shrek sighed. The only cause he cared about was *his* cause, the one to get Fiona back!

After dinner, Shrek went in search of Fiona. He found her in the weapons area, fiercely fighting the practice dummies. She wielded axes, swords, and knives with amazing precision — and she was blindfolded!

Sensing someone behind her, Fiona whipped off her blindfold and swung her axe in Shrek's direction.

"Hello," Shrek said calmly, a workout towel slung around his neck. "Don't mind me."

"What are you doing?" Fiona wanted to know.

"What does it look like? I'm getting ready for ambush action," Shrek told her. "Oh yeah," he continued. "I always like to quad my lutes and do some scrunches before an operational op."

Fiona stared at him, her hands on her hips. It was

clear this guy didn't know what he was talking about.

Shrek pointed to a strangely-shaped weapon. "This one taken?" he asked.

"We use that to clean the toilets," Fiona stated.

Shrek reached for another weapon.

"And we use that one to clean the thing we clean the toilets with," Fiona said.

Shrek picked up a third weapon. This had to be right, he thought.

"There you go, chief," Fiona acknowledged.

Shrek struggled to pick up the weapon. He had no idea what to do with it, but he had to do his best to fake it. Maybe if he impressed Fiona with his fighting skills, she'd pay some attention to him.

Shrek finally managed to heave the weapon right in the middle of a witch-dummy. Proud of his accomplishment, Shrek puffed out his chest, smiled, and casually leaned on the dummy.

Crash! The dummy fell over, causing Shrek to lose his balance. Before he could regain his footing, he crashed into another dummy, and another, and another, until he was lying on the ground, covered with dummies!

"Hey, Scott?" Fiona said, looking at Shrek.

"It's, um, Shrek, actually," he said.

"I know all this is a big joke to you, but we've lost everything because of Rumpelstiltskin," Fiona said.

"I know," Shrek said standing up. "So did I."

For a moment, Fiona was taken aback. Maybe this ogre wasn't goofing around after all. He actually seemed — well, sincere.

But Fiona had no time for sentiments. She had an army to lead and a battle to win. "You're going to get yourself killed at the ambush tonight," she told Shrek.

"I'll be fine," Shrek told her. "I think I can take care of myself."

"Well, let's see about that," Fiona said, throwing a shield into Shrek's arms.

Then Fiona lifted a battle hammer and charged towards Shrek. He lifted his shield in defence, but Fiona was too good. She soon had him pinned against a tree.

Shrek knew he had to prove he was a worthy warrior, so he grabbed another battle hammer that was sitting on the ground nearby. He swung the hammer towards Fiona and . . .

"Ow!" Fiona cried.

Concerned that he may have hurt her, Shrek let down his guard. "Fiona?" he asked worriedly.

But Fiona was only pretending. Taking this opportunity, she deftly swung the hammer at Shrek's head. Just before impact, he lifted his shield to absorb the blow.

Shrek smiled. He could be good at this if he tried.

On and on, Fiona and Shrek sparred. They used bigger and bigger weapons as they moved closer and closer together in battle.

When all the weapons were knocked away, the two continued in hand-to-hand combat. Shrek loved sparring with Fiona. And he could tell that he wasn't the only one.

Finally, they grabbed each other's arms. They were locked together, face-to-face. Shrek could smell Fiona's stinky breath and it made his heart beat even faster.

Just then, one of Shrek's wrist guards fell off and clanged to the ground, shattering the moment.

"I got it," Fiona said, breaking away from Shrek. "Give me your hand," she said, holding the wrist guard.

Shrek lifted up his arm, and Fiona began to tie the armour's laces. "The dragon goes under the bridge, through the loop, and finally . . ."

"Into the castle," Shrek continued, remembering how she taught their ogre babies to tie their laces.

Fiona looked up at Shrek. As Shrek gazed into her eyes, he could see the Fiona he had once known and loved.

Fiona blinked and pulled away from Shrek. "OK, good," she said, shaking her head as if she was waking up from a dream. "It seems like you can handle yourself."

"Fiona," Shrek started.

But Fiona was back to business. "Now go get ready for the mission," she commanded.

"I will," Shrek assured her. "But if I . . ."

"That's an order," Fiona asserted, turning on her heels and walking off into the night.

Chapter Seventeen

Shrek watched Fiona walk away and hung his head. As he walked past the other ogres getting ready for battle, all he could think about was Fiona. His mind was on the fight for *her*, not the fight against Rumpelstiltskin.

"Ogre! Un momento! Ogre!" Shrek heard someone call out.

He stopped and turned to see Puss In Boots scampering to catch up with him.

"I am not believing what I have just witnessed," spoke an awestruck Puss. "Back there, you and Fiona, there was a spark — a spark inside her heart I thought was long extinguished. It was as if, for one moment, Fiona had actually found her true love."

"I *am* her true love," Shrek insisted. "I rescued her from the Dragon's Keep. I was supposed to end her curse."

"Her curse?" asked a surprised Puss.

"By night one way, by day another," Shrek recited.

Puss gasped. "You even know the little rhyme," he said. "It is true, you are the one. You must prove it to her."

"How?" asked Shrek. After all, he had so far made two very valiant efforts, only to be rejected.

Thankfully, Puss had a fresh idea. "Go to her when she is alone," he said, "and tell her something that only her true love would know."

Shrek thought about Puss's plan. It just might work — if only he could figure out what to say!

🍄🍄🍄

It was ambush time. Fiona and her troops arrived at the mission site and waited for Rumpel to appear.

"I'll scout ahead," Fiona told Brogan. "Wait for my signal."

Fiona quietly and quickly scrambled up to her lookout spot. She peered out from behind a shattered turret wall, watching for any sign of Rumpel's carriage.

Then Shrek came up behind Fiona, startling her. "It's quite a view from up here," he said.

Fiona turned around. "What are you doing?" she said harshly. "Get back in position!"

But Shrek wasn't about to go anywhere. "You need to know once and for all who I really am," he told her.

"You're going to ruin everything!" Fiona shouted.

"Ruin everything?" Shrek shot back. "Actually, I'm going to fix everything. The ogres, Rumpel, your curse . . ."

Hearing that, Fiona whipped out a knife. "How do you know about my curse?" she cried.

Fiona was so busy reprimanding Shrek, she didn't notice Rumpel's carriage pass by behind her.

"Listen, I don't know who you are or how you know about my curse,'" she said, "but if any of these ogres find out that I'm a —"

"A beautiful princess?" Shrek finished.

"That is not who I am," Fiona declared. "Not any more."

Shrek could see that Fiona was upset. This was his

chance to prove his love for her.

"I know everything about you," he said. "I know you sing so beautifully that birds explode. I know that when you sign your name, you put a heart over the *i*. I know that when you see a shooting star you cross your fingers on both hands, squinch up your nose, and you make a wish," Shrek continued.

Fiona loosened her grip on Shrek, softening a little. Shrek continued.

"I know that you don't like the covers wrapped around your feet, and I know that you sleep by candlelight because every time you close your eyes, you're afraid you're going to wake up back in that tower," he said.

Fiona lowered her knife. She couldn't understand how or why, but this ogre really *did* know her.

"But most importantly, Fiona," Shrek concluded, "I know that the reason that you turn human every day is because you've never been kissed, well, by me."

Fiona looked into Shrek's eyes. Soft music began to play, and Fiona put her arms around Shrek's neck. Shrek smiled and put his arms around her waist.

Suddenly, Fiona dipped him — they were . . . dancing?

"You move fast," Shrek told her.

"It's not me doing the moving," Fiona said as the music started playing faster and faster.

All at once, Fiona and Shrek started tangoing down the hill.

"Why is this happening?" Fiona asked.

"Love?" Shrek ventured.

"No," Fiona insisted. "I'm being *forced* to dance!"

Fiona and Shrek danced and danced, until they met up with the rest of the ogre army. They were dancing, too, right towards Rumpel's castle. Surely, that schemer was responsible for this.

"I can't believe I let this happen," Fiona said as she and Shrek danced with the rest of the ogres. "And it's all because of you!"

"If you had just let me kiss you —" Shrek started.

"What?" Fiona was furious. "You're insane."

Then Shrek tossed Fiona into the air in a fancy dance move. This was one twisted tango!

Just then, Donkey arrived, pulling Puss behind him in a rickshaw. They saw that their friends were

under the spell of the Pied Piper. There was no doubt in their minds: Rumpel was behind all of this. The ogres had been set up! And the Piper's spell was working — the dancing ogres were heading straight into Rumpel's palace!

"We must do something before they fandango themselves into oblivion," Puss told Donkey.

But Donkey didn't know what they could do — he was dancing, too.

"When somebody tooties that flutey, I've got to shake my booty," Donkey explained.

Puss knew exactly what had to be done. He reached out and scratched Donkey right on his booty!

"Ahhh!" Donkey cried, rearing up wildly.

But that got Donkey into gear. Still pulling Puss behind him in the rickshaw, Donkey raced down the hill towards the Pied Piper and the conga line of ogres. He sped past the dancing fools until he reached Fiona and Shrek. Swiftly, he scooped them up and whisked them away from the enchanted music as fast as possible.

"Puss and Donkey to the rescue!" Donkey shouted.

Donkey was so busy racing away from the scene of dancing ogres that he didn't notice that he was fast approaching a high, and very dangerous — CLIFF!

"*Ahhhh,*" they all cried as they tumbled off the cliff towards a raging river below, splashing into the turbulent waters.

The group managed to get themselves to shore. Donkey and Puss were drying off, while Fiona was desperately trying to figure out a way to help the rest of the ogres.

But Shrek didn't want her to go; he knew it was far too dangerous. Rumpel probably had them all locked up by now. Suddenly, Shrek had an idea.

"Fiona, wait!" he cried after her. "Kiss me."

"What?" Fiona said.

"It's the only way to save your friends," Shrek insisted. But Fiona just continued to walk away, intent on saving her loyal army.

"There was a time in your life when you believed in true love and that a single kiss could solve everything," said Shrek. "All I'm asking is for you to believe that now."

Fiona stopped in her tracks. Slowly, she turned

around, walked over to Shrek, and gave him what he had been wanting — a big, fat kiss!

Fireflies swirled in the air. The wind blew through Fiona's hair (and over Shrek's bald head). Donkey and Puss stopped and stared, their mouths open in amazement.

When the kiss was over, Shrek opened his eyes.

But everything was exactly the same as it had been a moment ago.

"I don't understand," Shrek said. "The kiss was supposed to fix everything."

"Yeah, you know what? That's what they told me, too," Fiona said. "True love didn't get me out of that tower, I did. I saved myself. Don't you get it? It's all just a big fairy tale."

Shrek shook his head. "Fiona, don't say that. True love does exist."

Fiona was furious. "And how would you know that," she said, enraged. "Did you grow up locked away in a Dragon's Keep? Did you live all alone in a miserable tower? Did you cry yourself to sleep every night, waiting for a true love that never came?"

"But Fiona," Shrek insisted. "I'm your true

love."

"Then where were you when I needed you?" she shot back.

Her words stung. Shrek didn't know what to say. So Fiona simply spun on her heels and stormed away.

"Maybe you kissed her wrong?" Puss suggested after Fiona had left.

"No," Shrek said. "The kiss didn't work because Fiona doesn't love me."

Sadly, Shrek realized that as his day dwindled away, so did his chance of wooing his one true love.

Chapter
Eighteen

Inside Rumpelstiltskin's dungeon, the angry ogres were trapped in cages that were suspended from the ceiling.

"Don't despair, fellow ogres," Brogan said. "They can put us in cages, but they can't cage our honour!"

"I guess I should have cooked up some defeat-oritoes," Cookie added.

While the ogres were hopelessly hanging around, Rumpel was inside his palace, angrier than a hornet. Shrek had eluded them once more, as had the ogre army's leader, Fiona. It was time to fire the Piper.

"I've heard enough of your toot-a-lee-toot toots!" Rumpel yelled at the Pied Piper. "You blew it!"

Once the Piper was gone, Rumpel was ready to hatch his latest plan. He called for his speech wig. And his make-up. He was ready to address his royal subjects.

The giant Magic Mirror, hanging in a store window, summoned the villagers. "Attention, citizens!" it announced. "Please stay tuned for a message from our tyrannical dictator!"

A crowd of unhappy-looking peasants gathered, and instantly, Rumpelstiltskin's image appeared on the Magic Mirror's screen. It appeared as though he was standing in front of a beautiful blue sky.

"Hello, people. It is I, Rumpelstiltskin, shepherd of your dreams," he greeted. "It has been my pleasure to serve you, my loyal subjects, with top-notch service, affection, and protection."

The image behind Rumpel changed to a cloudy mountaintop.

"But recently, a certain somebody has jeopardized our joyous lives," he continued.

The image changed again, this time to a pebble beach at sunset. Then, suddenly, the background burst into flames!

"And that somebody is the rat-munching ogre called Shrek!" he concluded.

Images of Shrek and Fiona popped onto the screen of the Magic Mirror. More peasants gathered around

to look as Rumpel asked for their help in capturing the ogre.

"Whoever brings me this ogre shall receive," Rumpel said, pausing for effect, "a lifetime of happiness!"

"Just think of it!" Rumpel continued. "Total and complete happiness. All your greatest wishes! Your wildest dreams. Anything you could ever want. No strings attached!"

But time was short. Shrek needed to be captured before day's end. If not — the deal was off!

The villagers were intrigued. This could mean a new chance at life for gladiator Gingy. A chance at being a real boy for Pinocchio!

The villagers were determined to find Shrek and claim their prize. They gathered up their pitchforks and their torches and began the hunt.

"Shrek! Shrek! Shrek!" they shouted as they marched over a bridge—right over to where Shrek, Donkey, and Puss were hiding!

Unaware of the villager's search for Shrek, Donkey and Puss were trying to make the not-so-jolly green

ogre feel better. But nothing they said consoled him. He was becoming sure that Fiona would never love him before this day was done.

"Look, Shrek," Donkey said, "I know things might look bleak right now, but things will turn out all right in the end. Why, I bet by this time tomorrow . . ."

"Don't you understand?" Shrek interrupted. "There *is* no tomorrow! There's no day after that! And there's no day after that day after that! My life was perfect and I'm never going to get it back."

"If your life was so perfect, then why did you sign it all away to Rumpelstiltskin in the first place?" Donkey asked.

"Because I didn't know what I had until it was gone! All right?" Shrek shouted.

Then Shrek realized what he had just said. It was true. He had taken his life for granted. He didn't know how good he had it — until it was too late. And now he'd been trying to get his life back and had forgotten about Fiona. She had a new life now. And she was fighting to rid the land of Rumpelstiltskin. Although Shrek desperately wanted his own life back, he knew he had to help Fiona in her cause.

Just then, Shrek heard a little sound.

Thump! Thump! Thump!

Shrek, Puss, and Donkey looked around. What was that noise? And where was it coming from?

"Surrender now," Shrek heard a small voice call.

Shrek looked down to see tiny Gingy standing on the floor, trying his hardest to attack Shrek's foot.

"Don't try to fight it, ogre," Gingy said, trying to be fierce. "You're only making it harder on yourself."

Shrek laughed as he bent down to pick up the little biscuit.

"Unhand me, green devil!" Gingy shouted.

When Shrek asked Gingy was he doing, Gingy told him about Rumpelstiltskin's promise to provide the "deal of a lifetime" in exchange for capturing Shrek. And little Gingy was determined to get the deal of a lifetime!

Shrek put Gingy down on the ground. He knew what he had to do.

"Puss, Donkey, I want you two to stay here," he said.

"But I thought we were supposed to be a team," said Donkey.

"Not this time, Donkey," said Shrek. "This is something I have to do on my own."

"OK, Gingy," he continued, "now tell me about this deal." But when Shrek went to look for Gingy, all he saw were some gingerbread crumbs on Puss's mouth. Shrek and Donkey stared at the fat cat, stunned.

Puss had a guilty look on his face. "Oh, were you going to eat that?" he asked.

Shrek sighed. He was no longer able to get the information he wanted out of Gingy. But that wouldn't stop him from following through with his plan.

Chapter Nineteen

Back at the palace, the Three Blind Mice stood on a table in front of Rumpel. One of the mice wore a tiny, terrible-looking Shrek costume.

"Roar!" said the mouse. "I'm an ogre."

"Careful," another mouse warned Rumpel. "He'll make a sandwich out of your liver!"

But Rumpel was not amused. He dismissed the Three Blind Mice with a wave of his hand.

A huge crowd of villagers stood in line, waiting their turn to see Rumpelstiltskin and convince him they had captured Shrek. The Three Pigs showed up with Wolfie in an ogre costume. Butter Pants and Lemke tried to pass off a troll for Shrek. And Pinocchio even tried painting poor old Geppetto green.

"That is your father, painted green," Rumpel told Pinocchio.

"No, it's Shrek," responded the puppet. "Honest!"

It was clear this was going to be a long night. And Rumpel had no patience left.

"Can no one bring me Shrek?" he shouted.

"Stiltskin!" a big, deep voice hollered from the doorway. "I hear you're looking for me."

Rumpel looked up to see none other than Shrek standing in his castle. He was elated!

"Whoever turned Shrek in is going to get anything their greedy, little heart desires!" Rumpel declared. He pulled out the Deal of a Lifetime contract, looking around the room for the lucky person responsible for this.

Shrek grabbed the contract out of Rumpel's hands. "Being that I turned myself in, I guess that someone would be me," he said.

Rumpelstiltskin was stunned. He could only watch, speechless, as Shrek placed a bottle of ink on the table and plucked a feather from Fifi's fluffy bottom.

"The only thing my heart desires is to make things right again," said Shrek. He dipped the quill into the magic golden ink and hovered his hand above the Deal of a Lifetime contract, ready to sign.

But before Shrek could put pen to paper, Rumpel interrupted.

"Oh no, Shrek. Only true love's kiss can break your contract. So if you thought you were just going to do-dah-do-dah-do in here and get your life back—"

"I didn't," Shrek put in.

Rumpel's eyes grew narrow with suspicion. "Then what is it that you want?" he asked.

Shrek grinned. He put the pen to the contract and signed his name.

Outside the palace, there was a big commotion. All the "Ogre Wanted" posters tacked to trees and signposts disappeared into thin air. And the ogres that had been trapped in Rumpel's cages suddenly tumbled out of the sky, crashing to the ground.

"We're free? We're free!" Brogan and the other ogres shouted. They didn't quite understand how this had happened, but they were ecstatic to be liberated from Rumpel's dungeon.

"Where's Shrek?" asked Donkey, as he and Puss

turned towards the palace.

"This is not good," said Puss.

Inside, Rumpel summoned his witches. They put Shrek in chains and walked him into the dungeon, with Rumpel leading the way.

But Shrek did not resist. He was content in his choice to use his Deal of a Lifetime to free the other ogres.

"I've got to say, Shrek, that was some pretty heroic stuff," said Rumpel. "I should thank you for making my job so much easier."

"Except I didn't do it for you," Shrek told him. "I did it for Fiona."

"I bet Fiona would be really touched," said Rumpel. "I guess you can tell her that yourself," he added.

Shrek was confused. Fiona should have been freed along with the other ogres. But there she was, bound up in chains across the room from Shrek.

"Fiona!" Shrek shouted.

"Caught her trying to sneak into the palace through her old bedroom window," Rumpel said.

Shrek was furious. "Rumpel, we had a deal!" he boomed. "You agreed to free *all ogres*!"

"Oh yeah, but Fiona isn't 'all ogre,' is she?"

Shrek hung his head. Rumpel was right. Because her curse had never been broken, Fiona was only an ogre by night. By day, she was a beautiful princess.

"Nobody's smart but me!" Rumpel declared. All too pleased with himself, Rumpel left the room, slamming the dungeon door behind him.

Shrek turned to Fiona to see if she was all right. But when he tried to approach her, he was yanked backward. Rumpel had rigged their chains together so that they had to stay far apart.

Fiona looked at Shrek, and he could tell she knew the sacrifices he had made — for her and for the other ogres.

"I owe you an apology," Fiona said.

"No, Fiona," Shrek countered. "I'm the one who should be apologizing to you. I made a mess of everything." He sighed. "I'm sorry I wasn't there for you."

"Well, you're here now," Fiona said with a soft smile.

Fiona's heart was softening at last! But as night began to come to a close, it might have been too little, too late.

Chapter Twenty

While Fiona and Shrek were locked up in the dungeon, Donkey was trying to make his way into the palace. But the ogres weren't making it easy for him.

Cookie held Donkey by the tail, keeping him back.

"Let go of me!" Donkey shouted. "I have got to save Shrek!"

"Don't be a fool, mule," said Cookie.

"He's right," said Brogan. "Rumpel's palace is locked up tighter than Old Mother Hubbard's cupboard."

"Yeah," agreed Cookie. "And even that cupboard wasn't guarded by a whole bunch of mean, ugly, nasty witches."

"Hey!" a screechy voice shouted from above. "We

can hear you!"

The group looked up to see two offended-looking witches peering out of the palace windows.

"Sorry!" shouted Brogan apologetically.

To keep their plan a secret, the ogres formed a huddle around Donkey and Puss.

"We must get into the palace!" Puss insisted.

"Man, me and Shrek just busted out of that palace," Donkey said.

"How?" Brogan wanted to know.

Just then, Donkey caught sight of his reflection in Brogran's shield. *Shiny!* Donkey thought. It reminded him of something. He had an idea!

"The same way we're going to get in!" Donkey told the group.

Inside his throne room, Rumpel watched as his new disco ball was lifted up onto the ceiling. He was pleased to finally replace the one Shrek had ruined when he had escaped the palace.

"My new pretty ball!" he exclaimed. "It looked a lot bigger in the catalogue. I guess it will have to do."

Rumpel walked out onto the dance floor as music

began to play.

"Witches!" Rumpel announced. "Finally, the moment we've all been waiting for! The main event of the evening! I present . . . Shrek and Fiona!"

The dance floor opened up. The cavernous opening revealed a shackled Shrek and Fiona in the dungeon below.

The witches broke out in a chorus of boos when they saw their enemies.

"But now for the real entertainment," Rumpel said, as billows of smoke began to rise from one end of the dungeon.

"I give you a princess's worst nightmare, Fiona's old flame, the keeper of the Keep — Dragon!"

Two yellow eyes appeared through the smoke. Seeing this ferocious creature, Fiona went white with fear. She had spent years being imprisoned by this terrifying creature. And now, here she was again, at its mercy.

Dragon reared up on her hind legs and opened her mouth. At any moment, Fiona knew, Dragon would unleash her fire.

Then, suddenly, a singing voice rang out amid the

tension in the room.

Everyone looked up. There was Donkey, singing while standing casually on top of the disco ball.

"Donkey?" an amazed Shrek asked.

Donkey added, "And Puss . . ."

"In Boots," finished Puss as he joined Donkey.

As Fiona and Shrek watched in amazement, Puss tapped his heel on the disco ball.

TOOT TOOT-A-TOOT! came the ogres' call from within.

And before anyone could blink an eye, the ball exploded, and out poured the ogre army!

Instantly, the ogres started battling the witches. Surprised and horrified by the attack — not to mention the destruction of yet another disco ball — Rumpel tried to run for cover.

Just as an ogre was about to smash Rumpel with a club, a witch swooped down, whisking him away to safety on a balcony up above.

"Get them, witches!" Rumpel ordered.

Other witches gathered on the balcony, where they threw pumpkin bombs at the ogres below.

From the top of the disco ball, Donkey and Puss

watched the battle below. Suddenly, Donkey spotted Dragon, who had once more turned her attention to Fiona and Shrek.

Donkey and Puss knew they had to do something. Instantly, Puss used his sword to cut the rope that held the ball to the ceiling, releasing the ball into a free fall.

Puss and Donkey fell down, down, into the dungeon. They landed on Dragon's head and bounced off, landing in different directions.

Donkey stood up, dazed. What he didn't realize was that Dragon was right behind him, poised to attack!

"Donkey, woo her!" Shrek shouted, hoping that his friend could make Dragon fall in love with him, just like he had in Shrek's old life.

"Woo who?" asked a scared Donkey.

Dragon growled, and Donkey stiffened with terror. Slowly, he turned to face the beast behind him. But what he saw wasn't so horrible or scary. What he saw was — lovely! Donkey and Dragon slowly moved towards each other. Donkey puckered up his lips and leaned in . . .

. . . as Dragon bared her teeth.

"Uh-oh," said Donkey, just before Dragon closed her mouth around him!

Luckily, Puss thought quickly. He jumped onto Dragon's tail, stabbing his sword into it. And out flew Donkey from Dragon's mouth. He soared through the air, landing on the back of Baba's flying broom.

"Road trip!" yelled Donkey.

Meanwhile, Dragon was desperately trying to shake off Puss. She swung her tail across the dungeon floor, shattering stone walls and some of the pulleys that rigged Fiona and Shrek in chains together. With another big shake of her tail, Dragon flung Puss across the dungeon.

Thankfully, Puss landed right in Fiona's arms. But Dragon just reared back, unleashing a huge blast of her fiery breath at Fiona and Puss.

Flames flashed, and smoke filled the room. And when the smoke cleared — Fiona and Puss were gone!

Dragon looked around in confusion. Then she saw Shrek, still on the dungeon floor, grunting as he hoisted up a chain that held Fiona, who was still carrying Puss. Shrek pulled and pulled, and Fiona and Puss were carried higher and higher into the air, until they were suspended safely above Dragon's head. Shrek breathed a sigh of relief as soon as they were out of harm's reach.

But now Dragon had turned her fury on Shrek, and she charged at him. Running as fast as his ogre legs could carry him, Shrek managed to outrun Dragon and her snapping jaws, climbing up to where Fiona and Puss were suspended.

The two ogres used the chains that still connected them to swing up towards the empty ogre cages hanging from the dungeon ceiling, while Puss clung to Fiona.

Then Puss leaped off Fiona and onto a cage. From there, he was able to climb to the dance floor above, safely out of Dragon's reach.

Next, Fiona swung over to Shrek, and they clung to the same cage together.

But Dragon wasn't about to let them get away so easily. As she geared up for an attack, Fiona and Shrek jumped to another cage. Dragon barely missed.

Shrek and Fiona waited for Dragon to try and charge again, but she couldn't move. She was stuck,

her snout wedged in tightly between the bars of the cage!

Shrek nodded to Fiona and the two instantly jumped off their cages and swung around Dragon with their chains. Around and around they swung, making sure Dragon was securely tied.

"The dragon goes under the bridge," Shrek said running towards the left.

"Through the loop," Fiona continued, running right.

And finally, "into the castle!" they concluded together.

They did it — Dragon was captured. Now it was time to find Rumpelstiltskin.

Chapter
Twenty-One

The battle raged on.

Witches continued to pelt pumpkin bombs at the ogres.

A few witches managed to shackle Brogan with some chains, but he just used the chains to swing the witches around and around the room, dizzying them.

Cookie flung chimichangas at the witches, knocking Baba off her broom. Donkey, still hanging on to the broom for dear life, was left flying it.

Things were working in the ogres' favour until, finally, Rumpelstiltskin was surrounded on all sides. The entire army of ogres was charging him, attacking witches with water-filled frogs as they approached.

In a last-ditch attempt to escape, Rumpel jumped off the balcony, landing safely on Fifi's back. Fifi flew up and across the throne room, headed for a window.

"So long! Ha! Ha!" Rumpel called.

But Rumpel's excitement didn't last long. From the dungeon beneath, Shrek threw a skull shackle, which caught Fifi's leg. Bull's-eye! Fifi and Rumpel weren't going anywhere!

"Come on, Fifi! Go! Flap your wings!" Rumpel urged his pet. Fifi flapped wildly, but the chains were too strong.

"Witches!" Rumpel called desperately. "Close up the floor!"

But before they could act, Shrek tightly grabbed the other end of the shackle holding Fifi. Then he grabbed Fiona around the waist, and Fifi's forceful flapping hoisted them up out of the dungeon, towards the throne room.

"Come on, for Daddy! Come on, Fifi!" Rumpel cried, urging the bird upward.

Shrek and Fiona were carried out of the dungeon just in time, as the dance floor closed behind them. The pair stood on solid ground.

Then, with all his might, Shrek yanked his end of the chain. He tugged Fifi so hard that she began to flail wildly in the air, shaking Rumpel off her back.

"Fifi, no!" Rumpel cried as he tumbled into the air.

Down, down he fell — right into the arms of Fiona!

"Victory is ours!" Fiona shouted holding the little man up by the scruff of his neck.

The ogres cheered. Fiona tossed Rumpel to Brogan.

"Cookie," Brogan said, "it looks like we're having curly-toed weirdo for breakfast."

And with that, the ogres broke out into a wild celebration.

Amid the festivities, Fiona and Shrek found themselves alone for a moment.

"Hey, we make a pretty good team," Fiona told him.

"You have no idea," Shrek said with a smile.

Shrek looked out the window. The first rays of sunlight were trickling through. Holy roasted rat — it was morning!

Shrek felt a tingling sensation in his fingers and collapsed on to the floor. As he looked at his hand, his fingers began to fade away. Next went his feet, and then his legs began to disappear.

"Shrek?" Fiona said, looking at the disappearing ogre.

"His day is up!" Rumpel shouted from captivity. "His day is—" Rumpel was cut short when the ogre holding him squeezed around the neck, choking off his words.

"There has to be something we can do," Fiona said desperately.

Shrek smiled weakly at Fiona. "You've already done everything for me, Fiona. You gave me a home and a family."

"You have kids?" a confused Fiona asked.

"*We* have kids," Shrek told her. "Fergus, Farkle, and a little girl named . . ."

"Felicia," Fiona and Shrek finished together.

Shrek raised his eyebrow and looked at Fiona.

"I've always wanted to have a daughter named Felicia," she said.

Shrek reached into his vest and pulled out Felicia's Sir Squeakles toy. "And someday you will," he said.

Shrek looked out the window. The sun was streaming in stronger. His time here was almost over.

He looked back at Fiona and said, "The best part

of my day, Fiona, was falling in love with you all over again."

As the rest of Shrek began to fade away, Fiona leaned over and gently kissed him on the lips.

Then the last drop of sand fell in the hourglass. And Shrek was gone.

Chapter
Twenty-Two

The morning sun fell on Fiona as she stood there, stunned. Shrek was gone.

"Fiona," said Puss, interrupting her thoughts. "The sunrise . . . You are still . . . an ogre."

Puss was right. Normally, at sunrise, Fiona turned into a princess. Then, it dawned on her.

"True love's form," Fiona said, looking at her ogre hands. When she had been kissed by her true love, she had been saved from her curse. Now she would always be an ogre.

"Impossible," a shocked Rumpel said.

Fiona smiled. The kiss had worked after all. Shrek was her true love.

Then suddenly, the wind picked up, swirling around everyone. Faster and faster it blew. Ogres and witches began to crumple. Rumpel cried out in fear as the ogre who was holding him disappeared. Rumpel dropped to the floor.

Then, to his utmost horror, Fifi disappeared, too. *Poof!* In the blink of a newt's eye, she was gone. Then Donkey crumpled away, and Puss, too. Finally, even Fiona was gone.

"No!" Rumpel cried, as everything around him disappeared into the magic wind. And there was nothing he could do to stop it.

🍄🍄🍄

"*Roooooaaaarrrrr!*" Shrek opened his eyes to find himself back at the Candy Apple, roaring to a cheering crowd.

Shrek shook his head. Had it all been a dream?

"I love you, Daddy," Butter Pants said to his dad, Lemke.

Shrek looked around. All of his friends and family were there — just where he left them. Could it be that he really had his life back?

"Shrek, are you OK?" Fiona asked, noticing the strange look on her husband's face.

Shrek turned to Fiona and swept her up in his . "Of course I'm OK," he told her. "I have the best friends in the world, three beautiful kids, and a wife that I love more than anything."

Then Shrek walked over to his children and gave them each a big hug, too.

"Happy birthday, Farkle and Fergus," Shrek said.

"And, Felicia, sweetheart, I believe this is yours," he took Felicia's Sir Squeakles toy out of his pocket and gave it back to her.

Just then, Donkey appeared. "Hey, Uncle Shrek, how about giving my babies an encore?" he asked, pointing to his dronkeys who were flying overhead.

"Please, señor. Let us have it!" Puss put in.

The crowd chanted Shrek's name, urging him to roar once more. But instead, Shrek reached up to his nose and blew, making his ears trumpet like battle horns. *Toot toot-a-toot!*

Toot toot-a-toot! the ogre babies responded.

Everyone let out a wild cheer.

Shrek scooped up his children, and looked Fiona in her eyes. "You know, Fiona," he began. "I always thought I rescued you from the Dragon's Keep."

"You did," Fiona agreed.

"No," Shrek told her. "It was *you* that rescued *me.*"

Fiona smiled, and Shrek gave her a big, old kiss.

THE END